W9-BAQ-232

The Mystery
of Little Bear

To T.J. Schaaf
Merry Christmas, 2012

Bud
Cole

by

Bud Cole

Illustrated by

Deborah Miller

∞ INFINITY
PUBLISHING

All rights reserved. No part of this book shall be reproduced or transmitted in any form or by any means, electronic, mechanical, magnetic, photographic including photocopying, recording or by any information storage and retrieval system, without prior written permission of the publisher. No patent liability is assumed with respect to the use of the information contained herein. Although every precaution has been taken in the preparation of this book, the publisher and author assume no responsibility for errors or omissions. Neither is any liability assumed for damages resulting from the use of the information contained herein.

Copyright © 2012 by Bud Cole

ISBN 978-0-7414-8106-1

Printed in the United States of America

This is a work of fiction. Names, characters, places, and incidents either are the product of the author's imagination or are used fictitiously. Any resemblance to actual events or locales or persons, living or dead, is entirely coincidental.

Published December 2012

INFINITY PUBLISHING
1094 New DeHaven Street, Suite 100
West Conshohocken, PA 19428-2713
Toll-free (877) BUY BOOK
Local Phone (610) 941-9999
Fax (610) 941-9959
Info@buybooksontheweb.com
www.buybooksontheweb.com

Dedication

To each dog owner, past and present, that knows how great it feels to return home to a tail wagging, loving dog anxiously waiting behind the door to greet you!

Contents

The Mystery of Little Bear

Goose bumps appeared on Buddy's skin as he heard the eerie noise again. Whatever was making the noise was several feet away in the waist-high weeds. The noise was not terribly loud, but it was a sound he had never heard before. Why had he gone to the woods alone? He felt his heart pounding.

Should he run, or be brave and find out what was making the strange noise? Buddy knew the difference between bravery and foolishness, but his curiosity kept him from running. The movement of the thick, dry weeds indicated that the creature making the noise was moving in Buddy's direction. He had to make a quick—and hopefully correct—decision. He'd been told he has a vivid imagination, and here it was, running wild. Should he run too? Buddy was about to run like never before in his life, when all of a sudden, the weeds separated right in front of him!

CHAPTER ONE

A COLD WINTER HIKE

Eleven-year-old Buddy Sterner remembered that Sunday afternoon in February as if it were yesterday. Buddy is the only child of David and Elizabeth Sterner. He has chestnut brown hair and hazel eyes. A tuft of hair constantly stands up on the back of his head. Although he uses all kinds of hair goo to make it lie down, it pops right up again.

Buddy's mother says it's called a cowlick, but as far as he can remember, he was never that close to a cow. And if a cow had licked him on the head, he would certainly remember. Perhaps this lick from a cow happened when he was very young. There is a family story about visiting Uncle Gerry's farm. And Uncle Gerry did have dairy cows. Could that be where he got the cowlick? Was it so long ago that he can't remember?

Pappy Sterner calls his only grandson "Alfalfa." Alfalfa is the name of a young boy that appeared in movies called "Our Gang" many years ago. Like Buddy, Alfalfa had tufts of hair on the back of his head that would not lie flat.

Buddy's family lives in an average size house, built at the back end of a wooded acre bordering a Christmas tree farm in eastern Pennsylvania. A winding driveway with spruce trees growing along both sides connects his house to the country road. They do not have mail delivery. Each day they must travel to the Cherryville Post Office to pick up their mail. Their mail is placed in a mail slot inside the post office. Buddy usually runs into the post office to get the mail. He uses a special three number combination to open the mail slot door.

Buddy is about average height for his age. When he worries about being shorter than other kids, his mother says that it doesn't matter how tall you are, how you look, or what your abilities might be as long as you try to do your best. He is shorter than most of the girls in his class, but then girls do grow faster at this age.

Buddy hates being shorter than most of the girls, especially Shirley. Buddy secretly likes Shirley, but he never admits it! His friends tease him about "Long Tall Shirley." They sing about Buddy and Shirley sitting in a tree and the rest of the silly rhyme that boys like to use to tease their friends about girls.

With no brothers and sisters, Buddy often has to rely on his imagination to amuse himself. And he certainly has a great imagination! During his daydreams, he fights monsters, outsmarts evil enemies and rescues kidnapped princesses and other people who are in trouble. In his mind, Buddy makes the final touchdown to win a football game or slides into home plate to score the deciding run in a baseball game. He also imagines putting in the three-point basket at the buzzer for the Philadelphia 76ers and slapping the puck past the goalie as the seconds of the third period tick down to zero in a Flyers' hockey game.

Unfortunately, Buddy is not that successful in his real athletic pursuits. He's an average athlete. He is pretty good at everything that he tries, but he is not a stand out in any one area. When Buddy was issued his first baseball uniform, he rushed home, put it on, and modeled in front of his bedroom mirror. "I look great," he thought as he watched his prancing reflection. He pretended to scoop up some hard grounders and threw the ball all the way from center field to first base for an out. Then he leaped high in the air at the center field fence to rob an opposing player of a home run. Finally as he imagined pitching the first no hitter in his baseball league's history and the crowd was going wild--his mother called him for dinner.

Books inspire many of Buddy's daydreams. He loves to read and visits the library whenever his parents have the time to take him there. His favorite books are about sports, mysteries and horses. He and his friends often pretend to be the characters and act out the best parts of the books they have read. The boys also like to act out the movies that they see at the Roxy Theater in town. Most of his imaginary adventures are accomplished on horseback.

Pappy Sterner has promised to buy Buddy a horse for his twelfth birthday. Whenever Buddy gets excited and talks about the horse, Mom reminds Buddy that although his Pappy means well, he sometimes makes promises that he does not keep. But Buddy knows his Pappy will not let him down.

*   *   *

Returning to that blustery February day, Buddy had nothing to do. "Mom, I'm bored," he complained. "None of my friends are home today. Can I go for a hike in the tree farm?"

"Yes, but be home by dark and don't go anywhere besides the tree farm," replied his mom. One of Mom's rules when Buddy goes out to play is that he must always tell her where he is going. When she knows where he is and when he will be home, Buddy's mom does not worry about him. It was a cold, clear February day, and the weather forecaster had predicted cold temperatures for the afternoon and even colder ones for the coming night. Buddy put on his warmest coat, boots, and gloves. Although the sky was clear and the sun was out, it was certainly a very cold day to go hiking.

Mom continued her work in the kitchen as she gave Buddy special orders concerning the cold weather. "Wear your ski hat and your soft scarf that Aunt Edna gave you for Christmas. It will keep your neck warm." Buddy's mom works as a nurse in the emergency room at Cherryville General Hospital, so she is always concerned about how Buddy dresses for winter weather. "Are you sure you want to go out in this frigid weather?"

"Yes, I'm tried of sitting around the house." Buddy and his dad usually watched the NFL games on Sunday afternoons, but the Super Bowl was over and Dad was working on income taxes. A hike seemed like a good idea. "It's better to be warm and dry than to be freezing later on," Mom said.

"Be home before dark, be careful, and keep your hat on! Remember, do not go anywhere other than the tree farm and be extra careful if you go near the stream. If you get wet, you will have hypothermia before you know it," Mom reminded him as he went to the laundry room. Buddy knew hypothermia was a condition in which the body core temperature drops below what is needed for normal body systems to function properly. The symptoms are shivering and mental confusion. He had learned about hypothermia while working on one of his Boy Scout merit badges.

"I'll be home on time," he shouted back as he closed the side door and stepped off the small redbrick deck at the side of the house. Grabbing two camouflage-colored ski poles, he started on his winter adventure. Dad had spray-painted a number of old ski poles for the family to use as hiking sticks. Walking toward the back of the yard, Buddy pulled his scarf up to cover his cold nose. He already appreciated Mom's advice about dressing for the weather.

As he walked, Buddy thought about Dad's comments about kids dressing properly for the weather. Dad teaches seventh grade at the school Buddy attends. Dad often complains that his students seem to have no idea what to wear to school. The school has no enforced dress code, so students wear just about whatever they want to wear. Some kids actually wear shorts and sandals to school during the winter.

Buddy had heard his dad tell Mom that when he takes his students outside for a long recess the ones wearing shorts and sandals finally realize that winter is usually cold. He described how the students would dance around complaining about the cold. Mom replied that she thought Dad was being rather cruel, but Dad said that if some of his students were dumb enough to wear shorts in the middle of winter, then they had to suffer the consequences.

Buddy agreed that it was fairly stupid to wear shorts when it was so cold outside, but then the kids who wore shorts usually weren't the ones that followed the school rules or did much studying either. Buddy and his friends stayed away from that crowd of seventh- and eighth-grade hooligans.

The noise of his footsteps in the crisp leaves brought Buddy back from his wandering thoughts. Scolding squirrels scampered and chattered ahead of him, hinting that he was not a welcome guest in their woods. As he stepped onto the sunlit dirt road at the edge of the tree farm, he stretched his arms and wiped his watering eyes with a tissue.

The tree farm belongs to Jake, a chunky, jolly gentleman with a long white beard. It's easy to spot Jake on the farm because he always wears a bright red coat, hat and high black boots. Buddy thinks Jake is perfect for his job of growing and selling Christmas trees.

Jake has given Buddy and his friends permission to hike and play among the trees, but he also stressed that they be careful not to damage the tiny new trees planted next to each stump. The stumps are the remains of trees cut during previous Christmas seasons. One can only imagine what great joy and beauty those trees had brought to family homes throughout the area.

In the distance Buddy could see the Blue Mountain touching the sky. The view of the mountain to the north set his mind adrift again. He thought about the good times he had spent with Mom and Dad hiking on the famous Appalachian Trail, which stretches over twenty-one hundred miles from Maine to Georgia along the top of the Appalachian Mountains. He'd enjoyed the challenge of the rugged trail sections that wind across the high ridges of Pennsylvania. Occasionally, the Sterners had camped in the basic trail shelters scattered along the trail when they extended a hike overnight.

Suddenly the silhouette and calls of a red-tailed hawk caught Buddy's eye. The large bird was gliding above the tree farm, hunting for dinner. Buddy could tell it was a red-tail because of its wide red tail and whitish breast. Buddy approached the deteriorating walls of an abandoned barn as he watched the hawk disappear behind the tree line. He decided to hide behind the wall to watch for deer. He had seen deer in the area several times before.

What luck! After sitting quietly for about ten minutes, Buddy spotted three deer coming into Jake's cow pasture from the steep slope of Christmas trees off to his left, about thirty yards away. The old foundation was about forty yards from the stream. The lower pasture is where the cows usually graze, but due to the frigid weather they were sheltered in the warm confines of the barn. Buddy was motionless, pretending to play the statue game in which everyone has to freeze and not move. The deer could not see him.

He was partially blocked by one of the crumbling walls of the old barn. Crouching down on one knee to stay concealed from the deer's view, he peered through the old barn doorway. The deer grazed on the grass near the stream for several minutes, and the smaller deer were moving in his direction. Although Buddy was sure he had not been seen, the largest deer raised its head, looking toward the foundation. It appeared to sense his presence. The two smaller deer continued eating. After a minute, the large deer lowered its head and resumed feeding. Buddy was so close that he could see the little clouds of water vapor formed by their breath.

Buddy had not been this close to deer before. The largest one raised its head again, twitched its ears from side to side, wiggled its nostrils, and sniffed the cold air. Deer have an excellent sense of smell, and a slight breeze was taking Buddy's scent in their direction.

Stomping its left front hoof several times, the large deer raised its white tail to alert its companions to possible danger. As if to say, "Let's get out of here," it flicked its white tail. The other two deer followed suit by flipping their tails. Abruptly, the three deer raced away, crossed the stream and then disappeared among the hemlocks growing along the far stream bank.

The deer reappeared in the clearing at the top of the far hill. Stopping for several seconds, they looked back toward Buddy. Then they dropped from view below the horizon.

Buddy is always pleased to see deer on the farm. This trio appeared to be females, because they had no antlers. Buddy couldn't be sure though, because he knew that all male members of the deer family—including elk and moose—grow new antlers each year and then shed them sometime during the following year. Whitetails grow new antlers in the spring and shed them during the winter. Animals with horns keep the horns for their entire lives.

One or both of the two smaller deer could have been male deer born during the previous spring. Their antlers would not be visible in February. Young male deer, called button bucks, have a small knob under the fur where the antlers will grow. Fawns tend to stay with their mother through the summer and winter until new babies are born the following spring.

Whispering under his breath, Buddy began walking toward the stream. "I bet the deer were a mother deer and her fawns that were born last spring. I wish they had stayed longer. It was really exciting being so close to them."

Buddy had learned in science class that very few of the antlers that the male deer shed each winter are found while people are out and about exploring the outdoors. One reason for this is that rodents, such as chipmunks, mice, squirrels, and porcupines, chew on the shed antlers. Rodents' front teeth continue to grow throughout their lifetime, and chewing hard materials like antlers helps keep the rodents' teeth from growing beyond the lower jaw, which could restrict the animals' ability to eat. Also, antlers contain materials, which are important to a rodent's diet.

Before the holidays, Dad had bought two wooden deer from Mr. Rothrock, the school custodian. Rocky made the deer out of hemlock planks. Dad included the figures as part of his front yard Christmas display. He tied a large red bow around both of their necks. Dad's friend Gene had given him a pair of real deer antlers, which Dad attached to the top of the one deer's head. Then he glued a red Christmas ball on the front of the head to represent a nose. The deer were supposed to be Rudolph, the Red-Nosed Reindeer and his girlfriend. When his Dad (who was also an only child) did funny things like this, it made Buddy think that he'd probably inherited his vivid imagination from his father.

While the wooden deer were on display in the yard, squirrels had chewed part way through one antler. As Dad and Buddy put away the Christmas decorations, Dad had told Buddy that the chewed antlers were definite proof that rodents eat shed deer antlers.

Buddy had walked from his protected position behind the barn foundation and was beside the stream. He found ice crystals beginning to form along the edges of the bank and around some of the smooth rocks. The rocks resembled the tops of bald men peering out of the water to see what was going on around them.

Like most kids, Buddy enjoyed dropping sticks and leaves into the stream and watching them bob along on the surface of the gurgling water. Although it was a very cold winter, the stream's current was strong enough to keep the water flowing.

The stream was not very wide; an adult could easily leap across it in a single bound. Last summer Buddy and his friends had carefully placed large stones in the stream as a pathway so that they could cross the stream without getting their feet wet. (Jake had told the boys not to create a dam with the stones because the water would build up and flood the pasture.)

Using the two ski poles for balance, Buddy carefully stepped from stone to stone across the stream to the spot where the deer had disappeared into the thick hemlock trees. Buddy saw many deer prints pressed into the frozen mud at the stream's edge. Unlike the pointed hooves of the deer Buddy was able to walk along the top of the frozen ground without breaking through.

The late afternoon sun was creating a rainbow of colors as it reflected off the ice crystals on the bank. Suddenly, as Buddy stooped to observe the newly broken crust where the deer had broken through, an unfamiliar sound in the distance caught his attention. Turning his head toward the noise, he cupped his hand around his ear, hoping to hear the sound again.

Buddy was curious about the noise, but it worried him a little, too. He wished his friends; Gene, Mike and Chris had been able to come along with him. The Four Musketeers, that's what they call their little group, always have a great time exploring the farm--it is one of their favorite places to spend their free time.

CHAPTER TWO

THE STRANGE NOISE

Last summer the boys had camped overnight in an open area on the farm using tents and other equipment borrowed from their Boy Scout Troop, Troop #63. The troop met each Monday in the summer in the open lot next to St. Michael's Church on Maple Street in Pennsville.

Buddy and his friends are in the Black Panther Patrol, a small group of scouts from the troop. They work together on scout activities and compete with the other patrols, especially their rival the Bloodhounds.

On that last summer weekend before school started, the boys had built a campfire and roasted marshmallows. Buddy's best friend Gene had made up scary ghost stories around the flickering campfire. (Buddy thinks of each of his friends as his very best friend.)

Gene has a great imagination too. Gene wants to be an Olympic skier and a professional fisherman when he grows up. Buddy knows Gene since they lived next to each other in Pennsville. They had gone to kindergarten, first and second grades together, but Buddy's family moved to Cherryville following second grade. Gene's family moved into a home in the Cherryville area last year, so they have been able to hangout together again.

Mike, another best friend, had been in charge of making breakfast during the August campout. Buddy and Mike met when they first joined Cub Scouts and they have continued to be great friends. Mike made fried eggs in a frying pan made from a hickory branch and aluminum foil. This was one of the survival skills that the boys had learned from their Scout leaders, Bill and Bobby. Unlike most tree branches, a hickory branch is very flexible and will bend without breaking. The branch can be bent into a circle, bound with a thin piece of wild grapevine, covered with aluminum foil and used as a frying pan. The aluminum foil was one of the items in the survival kit that Bill and Bobby had taught the boys to carry, along with a pocketknife, safety matches, insect repellent, and a flashlight.

The eggs that Mike had cooked were slightly burned from the hot campfire, but the boys thought they tasted much better than the eggs served at the Fried Omelet Diner in town. Food always seems to taste great when you're camping!

Chris is the newest member of the Musketeers. He recently moved to the area from Tennessee. His parents own the local store where Buddy's mom and dad often go to buy items that they run out of between major shopping trips to the large super market in Pennsville. Chris joined the scout troop during the Christmas holidays.

Meanwhile back at the stream, the strange sound seemed to be coming from the direction of the tree line between the two old farm fields on top of the hill behind Buddy. "What could that be?" Buddy whispered. "There's nothing but weeds growing up there."

The farmer had not planted crops in the fields as far back as Buddy could remember. Dad often talked about his fear that a developer might buy the land and build homes or businesses. Too many fruitful fields were being used for buildings. Dad told the boys that someday in the not too distant future there might not be enough fertile land left for growing food.

Buddy and his friends liked to play in the weed fields. They would make little balls of burdock stickers and throw them at each other. Burdock stickers are covered with hooked spines that stick to clothing or an animal's fur. The burdock spines and the cloth stick together in the same way that the opposite sides of Velcro join together.

Buddy recalled how his dad, during a hike in that same area, had told the boys that some observant person probably noticed how the hooked spines of the burdock stickers stick to the little loops of material on clothing. That observation most likely led to the invention of Velcro--and a lot of money for the inventor.

"Maybe it was a guy named Mr. Velcro. Where else would such a weird name come from? Boy, if I had come up with the idea I would have called it *Buddicro*. Everything would be attached to something else using *Buddicro*. Notebooks, sneakers, straps, everything would be held together with *Buddicro*. Hmm, I have to be more observant if I want to become rich."

In the burdock game, if a sticker ball hits someone and it sticks to his clothing, that boy is out of the game. The burdock balls will not stick to smooth clothing, but they stick perfectly to old sweaters like those the boys wear during the game. When only one person remains, he's the winner. The game is like playing paintball, but with no cost involved. And as they played, the boys unintentionally were planting new burdock plants, which will provide the ammunition for future games and a good shelter for small animals to take cover.

Sometimes the boys accidentally startled rabbits and other animals from their hiding places as they ran through the fields. Buddy and his friends agreed with Dad. They hoped a land developer would not buy the fields and build houses on their wild play area.

No longer hearing the strange noise, Buddy began dropping leaves into the stream. He pretended that a curled dry chestnut oak leaf and a similar sycamore leaf were kayaks racing along on an Olympic slalom course. The finish line for the race was an old log lying across the stream about fifty yards downstream from him. When the kayaks had floated about halfway to the log, Buddy heard the unfamiliar noise again. "It sounds like a baby crying, but not a human baby," Buddy softly said to himself. A shiver shot up his back as the mournful noise echoed down to the stream once more.

Buddy's mind wandered to the late movie he had watched on TV last night. His parents had gone to a dance to support a hospital charity and his favorite "young-boy sitter," Jeannine, was staying with him. (Buddy prefers not to have Jeannine called his babysitter because, after all, he is almost twelve years old.) Even though

Buddy would like to stay home alone, he is always happy when Jeannine comes to the house to stay with him. She's a cheerleader at the high school, and Buddy thinks she's an eleven on a scale of one to ten. They have a lot of fun playing games and watching television.

Of course, the movie last night had taken place in a creepy old house on a dark and stormy night with lots of thunder and lightning. The main character's car had run out of gas, he had seen an old house in the distance and gone there to look for shelter and help. He knocked on the door using a loud metal knocker shaped like a wolf face. No one came to the door, but as he continued to knock, the door slowly opened with a scary squeaking noise, as if the rusty hinges hadn't been oiled for years.

True to most movies, weird music had started playing in the background. Jeannine and Buddy knew the movie's spooky music meant something terrible was about to happen. And then, without warning, something did happened. The man disappeared. And then something much worse took place. Buddy had fallen asleep! He never found out how the movie ended.

Now, listening to the mysterious sound coming from the weed field, Buddy found crazy thoughts racing through his head. If he went to investigate, he might disappear like the guy in the movie had vanished. He could end up spiraling through a time tunnel into a different time period, unable to return.

Buddy thought that if he did travel back into history he would like to be able to pick the place and time. Maybe he would discover a special dial so he could pick the year. But what time period would he pick? Maybe he could go back to the time of the Civil War. If he went to the Battle of Gettysburg, he might be able to do something that could prevent some of the pain and suffering. Perhaps if he went back even further in history, he could become a knight and join King Arthur as a Knight of the Round Table. His knowledge of the future would be very helpful like in the book "A Knight in King Arthur's Court."

To chase away his wild thoughts, Buddy said to himself, "Why are the people in movies so stupid? They always go into the creepy house, and then they run down to the basement or up to the attic where they can't escape. If they had any brains they would not go in the house in the first place. If my car ever breaks down, I'll run straight home to Dad and Mom as soon as the weird music starts!"

The cawing of a noisy crow brought Buddy back to reality. By that time, the chestnut oak leaf had approached the finish line in his imaginary kayak race. It was the more seaworthy of the two leaves that reached the fallen tree. Bored with the leaf races, Buddy decided to trudge up the steep hill to the weed fields, even though he was not quite sure whether he really wanted to know what was creating the weird noise.

By the time he reached the crest of the hill, Buddy was out of breath and perspiring from the steep climb. A slight breeze chilled him. He wondered whether he would hear the noise again. Had he imagined hearing the sound while he was playing along the bank of the stream? Perhaps it was just the wind howling through the tall pine trees at the end of the field at the top of the bank.

Foxes, raccoons, weasels, and many other animals live in the woods and fields, but most of them do not travel about during the daylight hours. Buddy had learned the term *nocturnal* in science class. It meant to be active at night. Last week, as part of an environmental unit on wildlife, Buddy and his class had learned the shapes and sizes of local mammal prints. Buddy had won the prize for matching the most mammals with the tracks they make. Identifying tracks in his yard and the surrounding countryside had become one of his favorite activities.

His teacher, Mr. Cruise, also had charts of local animals hanging on the wall at the back of the classroom. The students identified the animals using identification books. They wrote the answers on an answer sheet and turned them in to Mr. Cruise when they finished identifying the animals on each chart. Buddy was the fifth student to finish the birds of prey chart. It was a fun way to learn plants and animals. Working on the charts was like going on a hike, observing an animal and then using an ID book to find out what it was.

Buddy and his dad made plaster casts from animal tracks they found in their yard and on the muddy farm lane behind the house. They also searched for tracks along the stream. Buddy's dad was teaching an animal unit and had set up the casts in the glass exhibit case at the entrance to his classroom. He also placed the chewed deer antlers in the display.

As Buddy reached the first field, he noticed several tracks in the snow. Most of the snow that had fallen the previous week had melted, but patches remained in shaded areas. The small tracks in the snow were not tracks that he recognized.

"I wonder if the creature making the strange noise made *these* tracks. Boy, I'm glad the tracks are small," Buddy thought. Small tracks weren't as scary as very large tracks. Buddy didn't want to have an encounter with something *really* big!

The tracks in the snow reminded him of a fall day when the children had been prohibited from going out on the playground for recess. No one knew why the playground was off limits. All they knew was that the secretary had announced to all the rooms, "Teachers and staff should not use the playground until further notice." The announcement sure stirred up a bunch of stories about why the playground was closed. No one had imagined that it was because a raccoon had wandered into the basketball court through an open gate. Maybe the noise Buddy heard in the weeds was a sick animal, and an animal making weird noises on a cold February afternoon might be sick! As he continued walking along the edge of the field, Buddy expected spooky music to start playing.

CHAPTER THREE

RACCOONS, STRANGE TRACKS AND GROUNDHOGS

On "The Day of the Raccoon" at Washington Middle School, Principal Peterson had called Officer Z, the wildlife conservation officer, for the Pennsylvania Game Commission to come to the school to capture and remove the raccoon. (The kids had dubbed the officer "Officer Z" because his last name started with a "Z" and it was long and hard to pronounce.) Because raccoons are nocturnal, Mr. Peterson had been concerned about seeing one in the middle of the afternoon. He thought it might be sick or have rabies.

Most of the teachers had closed their window blinds so their students would not be disturbed and had continued with their planned lessons. Not Mr. Cruise, though. He had allowed his students to watch the event from the safety of the classroom. Buddy and his classmates had enjoyed a ringside view. It took quite a long time for Officer Z to capture the raccoon, which certainly hadn't seemed very sick as it ran around inside the fence surrounding the basketball court.

The overweight officer had closed the gate and approached the animal with a large net. As Officer Z took giant swings with his net, the confused raccoon had run this way and that.

Looking like an overweight tennis player, swinging a long-handled net instead of a tennis racket, the officer had chased the raccoon from one end of the court to the other. The raccoon stayed just out of reach as it quickly changed direction. The whole class had broken into laughter when the raccoon turned and darted between the officer's legs.

At times it had looked like they were playing football, and what a funny sight it was, watching the chubby linebacker chasing the masked tailback around the court.

About five minutes into the chase, Mr. Peterson had entered the basketball court. Closing the gate behind him, he had tried to help the officer. Thinking that the sides had become unfair and Officer Z now had the advantage, Buddy's class started cheering for the raccoon. The girls named the raccoon "Ringtail." The students began chanting, "Go Ringtail. Go Ringtail!"

"You have to watch quietly," Mr. Cruise had reminded them. Finally, with Mr. Peterson's help, Officer Z had managed to snare the raccoon along the edge of the fence. It looked more like the raccoon had accidentally run into the net while running away from Mr. Peterson, because Officer Z had been standing against the fence, breathing heavily, with the net resting on the ground (although that's not how Officer Z would retell the story later).

After the raccoon had been placed safely in a cage in the back of the Pennsylvania Game Commission truck, Officer Z had come into the classroom to talk to Mr. Cruise. Buddy and the rest of the students had listened as Officer Z and Mr. Cruise talked quietly next to Mr. Cruise's desk. There was not another sound in the room. The kids were allowed to talk softly to one another when a visitor came into the room, but that time they wanted to hear what was being said.

"Jim, this was a tough assignment. It took a lot of skill to capture that dangerous creature," Officer Z had said still breathing heavily and out of breath. He hadn't realized that Mr. Cruise and the class had watched the whole comical adventure from their window.

"Yes, I can imagine it was very difficult," Mr. Cruise had responded with a smile, winking at his students.

Officer Z had turned toward the students. "You can't imagine what I have just been through. There was a very big sick animal on your basketball court. I spent quite a long time capturing the dangerous animal, but I have carefully placed it securely in a transfer cage on the back of my truck.

"Girls and boys, never, let me repeat, *never* approach a wild animal, even if it appears to be tame. It may be very dangerous. If you see an animal demonstrating unusual behavior or notice a nocturnal animal wandering about during the day, be sure to call me or one of my deputies."

He continued, "My motto is, big or small, don't stall, give Officer Z a call!" That's when his cell phone started to ring. "It's probably someone who needs me to capture another dangerous animal. A game protector's job is never dull. You will have to excuse me; I must go to my truck and return this call."

He had turned around to wave goodbye to the class as he moved toward the door. He hadn't seen Ms. Kingcaid, Buddy's language-arts teacher, standing at the door with her hands on her hips. The officer bumped right into her. When she regained her composure, she shouted in a sharp tone, "Mr. Cruise, do you realize that your students are two minutes late for my language arts class?"

"Grab your reading workbooks and library books," Mr. Cruise had shouted. "We can't keep Ms. Kingcaid waiting."

Officer Z had excused himself as he squeezed past Ms. Kingcaid in the doorway. It was amazing both Officer Z and Ms. Kingcaid could fit in the doorway at the same time. They certainly were not built like skinny fashion models.

Smiling at the memory of Officer Z banging into Ms. Kingcaid in the doorway, Buddy was startled back to the present as the strange sounds suddenly became louder and closer. The weeds just a few feet away from him were moving toward him indicating that something was approaching.

Buddy's first thought was to run, but his curiosity to see what would happen was stronger than his fear. Moving back several steps, he spread his legs apart. He placed his right hand on his hip while holding one of the ski poles outward in his left hand like a sword fighter. As he watched, the wave passing through the weeds reached the edge of the field.

Whatever it was, it was coming closer and closer to Buddy. He felt his heart pounding, and he shivered uncontrollably. The hairs on the back of his neck stood up—in fact, all the hairs on his body seemed to be standing at attention.

Buddy's thoughts raced. He thought of the scary movie, the possibility of disappearing into thin air, and of running as fast as he could in the opposite direction. The best part of his athletic ability was running fast. He was near panic when a little ball of fur emerged from the weeds.

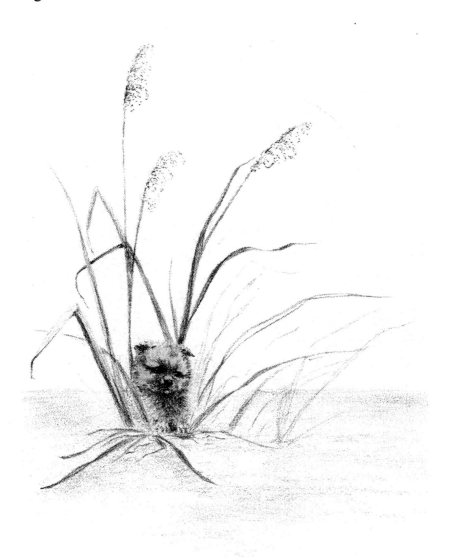

At first glance, it looked like a groundhog. But Buddy knew most groundhogs were still hibernating in mid-February, despite the popular Pennsylvania German story of groundhogs emerging to see their shadow on February second. Only the groundhog named Punxsutawney Phil--who was used in Punxsutawney, Pennsylvania to predict the rest of the winter's weather--was out in these frigid temperatures, and that was only because his handlers aroused him from his long winter's nap to attend the weather-predicting ceremony at Gobblers Knob. According to legend, if Phil the Groundhog sees his shadow on February second, there will be six more weeks of winter. If he does not see his shadow, the weather will become milder. Buddy's class had watched the TV coverage of the Ground Hog Day ceremony on CNN during class.

Looking carefully at the critter, Buddy realized that its paws matched those of the tracks in the snow. He studied the tracks again, but he could not recognize them as any he studied, and they definitely weren't groundhog tracks.

The little ball of fur looked up at Buddy, making the same sounds that had echoed down to the stream. Now, though, the sounds were much softer. Buddy could not believe that this little critter had created the loud sounds he had heard at the stream. "Oh no!" he thought. "Maybe this is the baby, but its mother or father made the sounds I heard before. Oh great, I know you should never come between a baby animal and its mother. Now what should I do?"

He took several steps back. The little fur ball followed him. Was it a baby fox or maybe a bear cub? It certainly didn't look like the animals he had studied in school, but as he tried to picture and match the tracks and the animal photos, he realized that the posters at school were all of adult animals. This animal appeared to be very young, in fact, too young to be out alone in the cold.

Whatever it was, it did not seem to be afraid. Amazingly, it kept following as Buddy continued to back away. He maintained his sword-fighting position. Reaching out with the ski pole, he cautiously placed the pole in front of the little critter. It was not afraid, nor did it turn and run. It just kept on coming, walking around and past the ski pole toward Buddy's feet.

Squatting down, he reached out with his glove-covered hand. Buddy knew his ski glove was thick enough to prevent a possible bite from penetrating through to his skin. Instead of a bite, the creature stuck out its little pink tongue, which was covered with several black spots, and began licking the glove. "What are you and how did you end up out here all by yourself?" Buddy giggled out loud.

Forgetting about the possibility of the critter's mother or father being nearby, Buddy carefully picked up the little furry animal. "Maybe it's a puppy of some kind. Are you lost? Did you wander away from your home?" Buddy asked as he held it safely away from his face at arm's length. Looking into the dark brown eyes of the little fur ball, Buddy began to giggle again. "You sure are cute, whatever you are!"

Buddy figured it was at least a half-mile to the nearest road or house. The sun was sinking low in the western sky. Buddy felt the chill of the increasing wind. The little animal in his hands was trembling from the cold. He had to make another decision. "It's too cold to leave you here in the weed field, but how will Mom and Dad react if I take you home? I remember what Dad did the time I brought the kitten home."

Several months ago Buddy had found a kitten in the woods between his yard and the tree farm. The kitten had most likely wandered away from Jake's barn. There are always stray cats around the farm, and they often have litters of kittens. That kitten had roamed up the hill toward Buddy's yard. Buddy was pretty sure it was one of Jake's kittens, but he decided to take it home instead of returning it to Jake's barn.

The next day, the school announcements had described the kitten and asked for a good family to adopt it. Following the announcement was David Sterner's name and room number. Kay Ann, one of the teacher's aides, had taken the kitten home to her family.

Buddy thought about what might happen if he took the furry little critter home with him. "Will Dad place an ad in the school announcements again or will Dad let me keep you for a pet?" Buddy said peering into the critter's dark brown eyes.

It was much too cold. Buddy had no choice, but to rescue the critter and take it home.

CHAPTER FOUR

GOING HOME

By this time Buddy felt confident that the little animal was not sick or dangerous. He also forgot that the creature's parents might be lurking nearby. Buddy carefully placed the shivering animal inside the opening at the top of his ski coat. It was time to head home.

The trembling stopped within the warmth of his coat. Was it fate that had brought Buddy to that area of the farm on such a cold day? The little furry animal seemed content to ride along inside Buddy's ski jacket. Buddy could feel its warm body against his chest.

"You poor little thing; how long have you been wandering around out here?" Buddy questioned. At least an hour had gone by between the time Buddy first heard the sounds near the stream and the time the little critter wandered out of the weed field.

It was almost dark. Buddy hurried along, concerned that his mom would begin to worry about him. As he headed up the hill through the tree farm, moisture from his breath settled on the furry head bouncing along just below his chin. Using the end of his scarf, he stopped briefly to wipe the moisture from the little critter's head. He didn't want his tiny friend to begin trembling again.

Zipping his coat a little higher, Buddy continued up the hill. Swaying back and forth within the warmth of the coat, the baby animal drifted off to sleep as quickly as Buddy's thoughts drifted off while daydreaming.

The sun was losing its grip on the sky and the wind was becoming stronger. The western sky was aglow with scattered clouds streaked with purple and orange, as if gently stroked with watercolors from an artist's paint brush.

The nearly full moon was high in the sky. The moonlight and the distant sunset reflected off patches of snow, making it easy for Buddy to find the small path through the woods. Tree branches creaking and rubbing against each other in the wind produced a ghostly sound in the moonlit woods. Relief and happiness washed over Buddy as he finally reached his own backyard.

He jumped into the air, landing on both feet at the same time, attempting to imitate the way Superman drops from the air to his feet in the movies. It was a maneuver that he and the other Musketeers often used when they entered a room or arrived somewhere. The sudden jolt caused the little fur ball to struggle to climb out through the top of the ski jacket.

Buddy could see his Mother's silhouette through the patio windows as he pushed the little critter's head back down into his jacket. Mom was in the kitchen preparing dinner. "What will Mom and Dad think of you?" he whispered to his new friend.

Thoughts of what he would say to his parents continued to race through Buddy's mind. He decided to sneak in through the laundry room, hide the secret bundle of fur in the garage, and figure out what to tell Mom and Dad later.

"It's about time you came home," his mother yelled to him as he closed the laundry room door and quickly headed for the garage.

"Yes, it's me, Mom. I'm going into the garage to take off my muddy boots," Buddy answered, rushing away before Mom could ask more questions. He had asked for a puppy for Christmas, but Dad had explained how a dog required a lot of care and training and how busy their family was with work, school, and other activities. There was no time for a pet.

Each time Buddy had asked for the special present, Dad said that a puppy requires a great deal of time and love, and it would not be fair for a puppy to be home alone all day while Mom was at the hospital and he and Buddy were at school. As a result, there was no furry present under the tree on Christmas morning--but now there was one in the garage!

Buddy has a ribbon snake named Slim and a gecko named Sam. They live together in an old thirty-gallon aquarium the family had once used for tropical fish. Like many families, they had lost interest in the aquarium when it turned green too often. Tropical fish are quite expensive and often do not live very long. Slim and Sam do not need much attention; in fact, they only need food several times a month.

Since they eat different foods, the two animals coexist without trouble in the aquarium. Sam eats crickets; Slim eats small fish and worms. Buddy thinks they are fun to watch, but he wants a pet he can play with. How can you play ball, take a walk, or wrestle on your bed with a snake and a lizard? Plus, Mom would have been very upset if he played with Slim and Sam on his bed.

When Mom and Dad had agreed to allow Buddy to buy a snake, and later a gecko, part of the agreement included keeping the aquarium in Buddy's bedroom where he would have full custody of the pets. Providing food, water, and keeping the aquarium clean are all responsibilities Buddy must fulfill in order to keep Slim and Sam. If he does not carry out his duties, the two reptiles will be looking for a new home. It would be a reason for Dad to place another school announcement indicating the need for someone to adopt a snake and a lizard in the same way that he had announced for a home for the kitten.

Several weeks ago Sam had lunged and grabbed Buddy's finger while Buddy was dumping crickets into the aquarium. The plastic bag full of two dozen crickets dropped to the floor. Crickets hopped for cover in all directions.

Dad and Buddy had caught nineteen crickets in small nets that Dad uses for stream ecology lessons when he takes his classes on nature field trips, but five of the crickets had escaped. Once in a while, very late at night, the missing crickets are still heard chirping somewhere in the far corners of the house.

Buddy came in from the garage and put his coat in the closet next to the laundry sink.

"I'm glad you're home! I was starting to worry about you," Mom said as she added freshly sliced mushrooms to the homemade spaghetti sauce that was simmering on the stove. The wonderful smell of the sauce filled the house. "Wash your hands and tell your dad to get ready for dinner too. I'm ready to drain the spaghetti."

Dad had finished working on the income taxes and was busy at his computer preparing a science test to give to his students on Tuesday. He does not give tests on Mondays, because he had hated Monday tests when he was a student. Dad told Buddy that he did not want to be a hypocrite and do things to his students that he hated when he was on the other side of the desk. He also had explained that a hypocrite was someone who tells someone not to do something and later does the same thing he says others shouldn't do. If Dad hated Monday tests and gave tests on Monday, he would be a hypocrite.

Buddy wished all teachers followed the no-tests-on-Monday rule. Ms. Kingcaid seemed to enjoy giving tests on Mondays. The kids think she purposely plans tests for Mondays so that it will ruin their weekends.

Buddy helped carry dishes, silverware, and food to the dining room. On Sundays, Mom cooks a special dinner, and the family eats at the antique oak table in the dining room instead of at the small table in the kitchen, which is their usual gathering spot during the week.

The spaghetti and meat sauce tasted fantastic after Buddy's cold afternoon adventure. A mixed-greens salad with Caesar dressing and fresh Italian bread topped off the healthy meal. Mom was always concerned about serving a well-balanced diet. She made sure her meals included foods from each level of the food pyramid.

Mom was discussing how the ingredients in the sauce were all from the family garden. She always named what garden veggies were part of her meals. She was very proud of her garden.

Buddy almost forgot about his secret in the garage--until unfamiliar sounds came from that direction.

"Did you hear something?" Dad asked.

Buddy quickly interrupted. "I didn't hear anything!"

Mom added, "It sounds almost like a dog barking."

Buddy shouted, "There is nothing in the garage," hoping to drown out any more sounds from that direction.

"There is no need to raise your voice at the table," Mom cautioned.

"I didn't realize I was shouting," Buddy continued at a loud volume.

"I know I didn't hear nothing!"

Mom corrected Buddy's grammar. "You know not to use a double negative in the same sentence. You can't use didn't and nothing in the same sentence. You need to say I didn't hear anything."

"That's right, I didn't hear anything. You and Dad must be hearing things. Can I have more sauce on my spaghetti," he yelled, trying to keep the conversation away from the noise. "I just love your garden veggie sauces."

But Dad continued on about the noise. "I can't quite make out what it is. It sounds like a cat or maybe a dog whimpering."

The noise stopped, and the conversation turned back to the day's events. Dad enjoyed having family conversations at the dinner table. During the dinner table discussions, each member of the family told the other members about what they had done that day.

"Do you know that many family members at school do not know what the other members in their family are doing most of the time? Everyone is so busy they don't even eat at the same time anymore. My family always ate together, and as long as possible, I want the three of us to sit down and eat together too," Dad explained.

"I totally agree," Mom responded. "Unless I have a work shift at mealtime, we need to eat together."

Pappy Sterner, Buddy's grandfather, never allowed talking during mealtime. When someone began talking he always said that he wanted peace and quiet while he ate. He had worked in the noisy foundry at the Bethlehem Steel Company and heard loud noises all day. He didn't want anything distracting him at the table.

Nana and Pappy Sterner had lived with Buddy and his parents for several months last year after Pappy retired. They sold their home and needed a place to live until their new townhouse in Florida was completed. Buddy loves his Pappy and Nana, but Pappy is very strict. Buddy's father uses many of Pappy's rules and ideas with Buddy. Now that Buddy's grandparents live in Florida, Buddy only sees them several times a year. Usually they come to visit during the Christmas or Easter vacation.

All of a sudden the noise from the garage started again, louder than before. Dad stood up. "I'm going to check the garage. Perhaps a cat or something came in when the door was open."

Buddy jumped to his feet. "I'll go check out the garage," he yelled. "You sit and relax. Maybe it's the neighbors' black cat, Spooky! Maybe he followed the car into the garage before the door closed." Spooky liked to sit on the hood of the car to keep warm. Dad was not happy whenever he found muddy cat tracks on the car or van. He's very fussy about his vehicles and did not want to discover cat-claw scratches in the paint.

"If it is that cat, it better not be on the hood of Mom's car," Dad yelled sharply. "If he is there, open the door, grab the broom and chase him out!"

"I will," Buddy shouted back as he ran through the kitchen on his way to the garage.

CHAPTER FIVE

A SUDDEN SURPRISE

Buddy opened the door between the laundry room and the garage. The furry creature was sitting on the top step. Somehow it had escaped from the upended empty cardboard box in which Buddy had punched breathing holes to contain his little friend.

Before he could grab it, the furry animal streaked between Buddy's legs, heading straight for the dining room. Buddy followed in quick pursuit. It looked like the cat was out of the bag, as the old saying goes, or more accurately, that the fur ball was out of the garage. At least "The Great Garage Escape" solved one problem; Buddy no longer needed to figure out a way to explain his secret to Mom and Dad.

By the time Buddy reached the dining room, his mother was standing on her chair shouting, and Dad was standing next to his chair shaking his head with a puzzled look on his face. They were more surprised than frightened. The unexpected visitor had caught them off guard.

"What is that?" Mom shouted.

While the little critter hid trembling under the chair below the cuckoo clock in the corner of the room, Buddy excitedly explained how he found it near the edge of the weed fields at the far end of the tree farm.

"I was …down at the stream … below what's left of the old farm barn. Then I was …racing leaves …in the stream … when..."

At that point, Mom climbed down from her chair. "Buddy, sit down. Take a deep breath and try to relax," she said calmly.

Buddy took her advice. He sat down, took a deep breath, then jumped to his feet again, continuing his story as fast as a boy his age could talk, grabbing quick gasps of breaths between each sentence. "I heard a weird noise... coming from the weed field on the top of the hill." Gasp. "You know... the one where my friends and I like to play." Gasp. "When I went to investigate, it came out of the field." Gasp. "It's too cold to leave it out there." Gasp. "It's too little... it couldn't spend the night alone." Gasp. "It's so cute... it was trembling from the cold and it..."

Mom interrupted again. "Please slow down, sit down, and take another deep breath."

"Yeah," Dad commented, "You sound like an old 45 record playing at a higher speed." Buddy had no idea what Dad was talking about, but then his dad often referred to things that Buddy didn't understand.

Buddy settled down and quickly finished his explanation of the afternoon adventure. Then Mom, Dad, and Buddy attempted to capture the little fur ball. It was still curled up under the chair. Dad tried to place an old towel around it to avoid a possible scratch from its claws.

As Dad reached under the chair, the animal took off toward the kitchen. Even though it did not have very good balance, it continued to elude capture. They finally trapped it when it lost its balance in the corner of the laundry room. Dad used the old towel to pick it up and carefully placed it in the laundry sink. The little critter was too small to crawl out of the deep sink--at least, that was what Dad thought.

Mom found Buddy's ragged old baby blanket in the rag pile and spread it out on the bottom of the sink. Grabbing an old heavy tabletop from the garage, Dad placed it over the sink, leaving one edge open for air. "That should keep you out of trouble for the rest of the night," Dad said.

"Honey, I thought I threw that old tabletop away several weeks ago. How did it get back in the garage?" Mom asked.

"I guess it is a magic table," Dad replied.

"Can I keep it as a pet?" Buddy begged.

"Why do you want to keep an old tabletop for a pet?" Dad said, with a big smile on his face.

"Not the table, the puppy or whatever it is!"

"I don't think that that is a very good idea, you know very well that our busy schedule allows no time to care for an animal," Dad answered. Buddy's excitement was crushed.

Buddy's mom had owned a dog named Brandy back before Buddy was born, and she still missed Brandy, even though it was many years ago. Tears would fill Mom's eyes when she talked about Brandy. "I must figure out a way to have Mom fall in love with the little fur ball like she did with Brandy," Buddy whispered to himself.

Mom and Buddy tried to decide what kind of critter was staring up at them between the edge of the sink and the tabletop.

"How about Little Bear," Buddy said, "I think it looks like a little bear." The little fur ball finally settled down in the bottom of the sink.

After some discussion, Mom agreed. "I think Little Bear is a good name for it," Mom replied as she took the bath towels from the dryer and began folding and placing them on the top of the washing machine.

Dad's scientific mind kicked into gear. "It has a little tail, so it can't be a bear. Bears don't have noticeable tails."

"I still like the name Little Bear even if it does have a tiny tail."

Little Bear it would be, at least until they figured out what to do with it. Dad didn't say much more. He just stood by the laundry sink shaking his head. Buddy thought he detected a slight smile on Dad's face.

Buddy thought that his detecting a slight smile on Dad's face was a good sign. "We gave my little friend a name. Dad didn't even give me time to give the kitten a name. And I think Dad was smiling at Little Bear."

"Buddy, you clear the table and fill the dishwasher while I finish folding these towels," Mom said as she pulled more towels from the dryer. Dad slipped away to finish the science test he was preparing on the computer.

"Little Bear is the name of the Indian in the book *The Indian in the Cupboard* that we are reading in class this month," Buddy called to Mom as he filled the dishwasher with the dirty spaghetti dishes.

"Be sure to rinse the sauce from the dishes. That old dishwasher has trouble cleaning dry spaghetti sauce from the plates. Honey, we need to buy a new dishwasher. Now, where did your Dad go…?" Mom's voice tapered off as she realized Buddy's dad wasn't nearby.

After the towels were folded and the dishes were stacked in the dishwasher, Mom poured a small amount of Cheerios into a dish and warmed a cup of milk in the microwave. She added and stirred in the warm milk until the little oat circles softened. She tested the temperature of the milk on her arm. Buddy slid the tabletop to the side and lifted Little Bear from the sink. He placed him on the floor next to the milk and Cheerios. Little Bear started lapping up the milk and sucking down the Cheerios as if he had not eaten for quite some time.

"He sure is a hungry little fellow." Mom said with a smile.

"You mean a hungry little bear, don't you?" Buddy asked.

"I guess so."

Little Bear had his first warm meal in what Buddy hoped would become his new home. Mom picked up the pup and carefully placed him back into the sink. The little pup looked very content snuggling against Buddy's baby blanket.

Buddy didn't sleep very well that night. He kept going downstairs to check on Little Bear. The first two times he checked, Little Bear was sleeping soundly. Buddy stared into the sink watching his new and hopefully permanent friend as it slept. He kept checking to see if it was okay. Little Bear was getting plenty of rest, but Buddy was awake most of the night.

The third time he went to check the sink the tabletop was moved slightly to the side and Little Bear was gone. Buddy knew the little critter had to be somewhere in the house. He grabbed a flashlight and started a careful silent search, not wanting to wake his parents by turning on the lights or making any noise. There was no sign of the pup on the first floor and the basement door was closed, so it couldn't have gone down there. As Buddy reached the seventh step on his way to search the second floor, Little Bear surprised him. The little pup tumbled down the carpeted stairway like a fur-covered Slinky.

Meeting Little Bear on the stairs startled Buddy so much that he shouted and dropped the flashlight. His shout, the thud of the flashlight dropping, and the sound of it rolling down the steps woke up Mom and Dad.

"What in the world was that?" Mom shouted as she and Dad sat up in bed at exactly the same time. In what seemed like a "Beam me down, Scotty" scene from the old Star Trek shows, Buddy, Mom and Dad were standing together at the bottom of the stairs staring at Little Bear.

"You sure are a pain in the neck. Now you are ruining our night's sleep," Dad said as he stooped to pick him up. Before Dad could grab him, Little Bear ran off toward the dining room. Dad, Mom, and Buddy were right behind him. Buddy dove for the pup at the doorway, but despite its clumsy movements, Little Bear dodged away from Buddy and headed through the kitchen to the laundry room.

Dad grabbed the same rag towel that he had used to capture the fur ball the previous evening, but the pup was too quick and darted around Dad's bare feet on its way back to the dining room.

There must be something comforting about the ticking of a cuckoo clock, because Little Bear ran into the same corner under the chair where he had curled up when he first ran in from the garage. The trio surrounded him. All three had a rag towel. Mom grabbed the trembling fur ball, but she only seized hold of one back leg. Somehow Little Bear was able to squirm loose. This time Dad was there to snare it with his towel. The cuckoo cooed four times as mom carefully placed Little Bear back in the sink.

"This time it won't get out. I'm putting a twenty-five-pound barbell weight in the middle of the tabletop. It won't escape this time," Dad mumbled as he carefully placed the weight on the tabletop, allowing an inch or two of space for air between the side of the sink and the edge of the tabletop.

"It's after four. We need to get some sleep or we will be a bunch of crabby individuals tomorrow morning," Mom said with a yawn.

"What do you mean, tomorrow morning? It is morning," Dad grumbled as he headed toward the stairs.

Although he was very tired, Buddy jumped out of bed and bounded down the stairs about half an hour before the alarm was set to go off. He covered several steps at a time, feeling more excited than on a Christmas morning. When he ran into the laundry room, it felt like his heart dropped on the floor. The tabletop was pushed to the side and the pup was gone again. "How could Little Bear move twenty-five pounds and get out of the sink?" Buddy thought.

Buddy was very upset that Little Bear was not there. "Does this pup have magical powers or was it all a dream?" Frantically Buddy searched the house. He checked the closets, the basement, and the garage, and then he began to panic.

The shower was running and he could hear Dad singing. Dad always sang some Italian song about "old salami" or something like that. For some reason, people like to sing in the shower. Maybe they're bored or maybe they think no one can hear them. Buddy always knew when Dad was taking a shower by the loud and somewhat poor singing coming from the bathroom.

"Oh no, I hope Dad didn't get up early and take Little Bear to the lost animal place. He sounds pretty happy singing about the salami."

Mom was missing too. Buddy's imagination kicked into gear. Both Mom and Little Bear were missing. "Oh no, I bet they were both kidnapped during the night and they are being held for ransom money. I will have to bake cookies using Aunt Edna's cookie recipe and shovel snow to earn enough money to pay the ransom to get them back. First I will have to quit school and get a job and then..."

Lost in his thoughts, he sadly walked over to the sliding glass patio door. As he peered out through tear-filled eyes, he spotted Mom. She was in the backyard slowly walking backwards. She was still dressed in her robe although she had her long ski coat and she was wearing her fur-lined boots. And there was Little Bear following at her toes.

"Wow, it wasn't a dream! They weren't kidnapped either!" Seeing Mom and the pup made Buddy very happy. He could see a big smile on Mom's face. She was having a great time playing with Little Bear in the yard. "I guess this means I don't have to quit school, although I wouldn't miss it."

"Yes, all right, excellent!" He shouted out loud as he gestured with his arm and raised his right leg, bending it at the knee like professional golfers do when they sink a long putt or win a tournament. It was a perfect signal. "Mom likes him, Mom likes him!" Buddy shouted.

A light dusting of new snow covered the lawn. Buddy rolled back the sliding patio door and ran out into the yard to greet Mom and Little Bear. He had on his pajamas. As he ran barefoot into the yard, Mom quickly yelled and motioned for him to get back inside. "You'll freeze your toes off!" she shouted. But Buddy never heard Mom's warning. He was too intent on reaching Little Bear.

By the time he reached Mom and the pup, his feet were so cold that he seemed to be doing a strange dance. Jumping on one foot, then the other, then lifting his leg and grabbing his foot with his hand, Buddy frantically tried to warm his feet a bit. His dance resembled the description that the author of the Indian in the Cupboard used to describe Little Bear doing a war dance around his campfire.

Buddy quickly followed Mom to the laundry room door. Little Bear was between them. Its little legs were too short to crawl up onto the step. Buddy placed his half-frozen bare foot under the pup's little butt, gave it a lift and followed it into the laundry room. The pup was so young that it frequently toppled over to one side as it tried to run.

Dad was in the kitchen when Little Bear tumbled in. Dad began laughing as the fur ball did a somersault across the kitchen floor.

"You sure are a little character!" Dad chuckled as he poured another cup of coffee.

"Buddy, you better hurry and get ready so you don't miss the bus!" Mom shouted, bending over to pick up Little Bear. "You're so cute, yes you are, yes you are," she said holding the animal in front of her, shaking it gently back and forth and talking as if Little Bear were a little baby.

Buddy rushed upstairs to his bedroom. He brushed his teeth, dressed, flew back down to the kitchen, and gobbled down two waffles and some orange juice. Then he grabbed his coat, ski hat, and his book bag. Heading out the door, he stooped to pet Little Bear.

Running down to the bus stop, Buddy thought it would take forever until he was running back up the driveway at the end of the day. He also thought about how Dad laughed when Little Bear tumbled into the kitchen. That was another excellent sign that Dad might give in and allow Buddy to keep the pup.

The big yellow school bus with its blinking lights pulled to a stop near the Sterner's mailbox. Its long black-and-yellow-striped arm came out from the front bumper. Jerome, the bus driver, opened the door. Buddy climbed the two steps, gave a big smile to Jerome, patted the driver on his bald head and skipped to his seat. Buddy was in a very good mood.

CHAPTER SIX

LITTLE BEAR GOES TO SCHOOL

The school bus headed down the state highway as Buddy looked out the back window toward his house, where poor Little Bear was about to spend the day alone. Soon, Jerome maneuvered the bus into the lot in front of Marty's Market. Chris was standing on the market steps.

Buddy was eager to tell Chris about finding Little Bear. He started shouting as soon as Chris entered the bus. "Quick, hurry up!" Buddy shouted. Jerome does not allow yelling on his bus; Buddy could see Jerome giving the old evil eye in the large mirror hanging above the front windshield. Buddy signaled Jerome with a friendly nod and a wave of his hand to show that he got the hint. Chris quickly walked back to their seat and sat down. Softly but excitedly, Buddy told Chris the whole story about his afternoon adventure in the tree farm.

As the yellow bus full of students bounced along the back roads to Washington Middle School, Mom and Dad were discussing what to do with Little Bear. They could not leave him in the sink. The best option seemed to be for Dad to take him to school for the day. Mom could not take Little Bear to Cherryville Hospital, but Dad could keep an eye on him at school.

Mr. Peterson, the school principal, is also one of Buddy's father's friends. They taught together before Mr. Pete, as the teachers call him, became a principal. He loves dogs and has his own hunting dog, named Gunner. Dad felt confident that Mr. Pete would not be upset if he took the pup to school.

The decision was made. Mom rushed off to the hospital, leaving Dad to take care of the pup's needs. Dad took Buddy's baby blanket from the laundry sink and placed it in the bottom of the white oak pack basket that he uses to carry field trip equipment. Next he carefully put Little Bear in the basket on top of the baby blanket. In no time at all, they were on their way to school.

After parking his car, Buddy's father swung the pack basket over his shoulder and walked to the main office to talk to Mr. Peterson. The door to Mr. Pete's office was open. Dad peeked in and knocked softly on the door. Mr. Pete was at his desk working on inclement weather schedules.

"Do you have a minute, Pete?"

"What's in the big basket, your lunch?" he said, smiling. "Maybe you should cut back on your calorie intake."

"No, Buddy found this little critter at the edge of the weed field at the east end of the Christmas tree farm yesterday afternoon." Dad sat down and explained the story and how he and Elizabeth had no other choice but for him to bring the little critter to school.

"I have no problem with you bringing it to school with you. You couldn't leave it alone all day. It sure appears to be very young. What do you plan to do with it?" Mr. Pete asked as he peered into the basket.

"I haven't really given thought to that. I'm just taking things one step at a time."

"It's a cute little thing. Wow, look at the big paws. It's going to grow into a big dog."

Once he was assured that Pete was okay with the fact that the pup would be in school all day Buddy's dad went back out into the office lobby and placed the pack basket on the floor while he checked his mail. Teachers and other staff members stopped to pet the friendly little critter as they came into the office to check their mailboxes. Mr. Pierzga was especially interested in Little Bear. The teacher had had to put his beloved hunting companion, Champ, to sleep last spring. Champ, his Brittany spaniel, was thirteen years old. Mr. Pete and Mr. Pierzga had spent many days hunting together with Champ and Gunner.

Everyone wanted to know more about Little Bear. Dave Sterner told the story several times as new staff members entered the office. He decided to ask Mr. Pete's secretary, Grace, to add a brief description of Buddy's tree-farm adventure to the written daily announcement sheet that teachers received in their office mailbox at the beginning of each day. In that way all the staff would know why Little Bear was in school. Grace was almost finished with the original copy.

Mrs. Ross, the school librarian, entered the office. "What a cute pup. When did you add a new addition to the family?" she asked.

"Grace is typing a brief description for the morning announcement sheet. I don't want to be rude and not answer you, but I have to get to my classroom. The buses have arrived and the kids will be coming in soon and I have some work that I need to write on my chalkboard. Why don't you peek over Grace's shoulder as she finishes typing the information?"

Buddy's dad left the basket and Little Bear at the edge of Grace's desk and went to his room. The staff members in the office began chattering about how the pup might be the offspring of a wild animal. A wolf, fox, bear, and coyote were mentioned as possibilities. Mr. Pierzga, who works with the special-needs children, went to the library to look for reference books containing information on the four kinds of animals mentioned during the office conversations. He decided to eliminate wolf from his search because he knew that there were no wild wolves in Pennsylvania.

While staff members were checking mail and messages, Mr. Pete entered from his office and gave his opinion. "I figure it's a mixed-breed puppy that was dropped off near the tree farm by someone who did not want to care for it."

"That's a cruel possibility, considering how cold it was last night," Grace exclaimed. "The temperature was about eight degrees. That's really cold. My dog didn't want to go out for his final walk last night because of the freezing temperature." The general opinion was that the pup would not have survived the frigid temperatures if Buddy had not come to the rescue.

Mrs. Ross used her library computer to look for pictures on the Internet that might resemble Little Bear. Soon the news of Little Bear and Buddy's story spread throughout the school. Several teachers waiting to use the copy machine in the copy room were talking about the little visitor that Dave Sterner brought to school.

At eight thirty, the school bell rang to announce the beginning of a new school day and a new week. As the bell rang, the bus students noisily entered the main doors in front of the office. Mr. Zalutsky was on bus duty for the week. He teaches eighth-grade English and is the ski club advisor. The students quieted down when they saw him. He has a reputation for being very strict.

Mr. Zalutsky is especially stern about noise in the hallways. No one messed around when he was on duty. The kids think he has a fake hand, because he often bangs the back of his hand against the chalkboard when he becomes upset about classroom behavior. Very few students dare to come in unprepared to eighth-grade English classes and if they try it once they never try it again.

Tall and lanky, eighth grader Barbara Corbo spotted Little Bear in the pack basket when she stopped in the office to pay back the lunch money she owed from last week. She has a poor memory-- unless it has to do with gossip. While Barbara forgets her lunch money at least once a week, she never forgets to pass on good gossip. When Barbara finds out something, it's like announcing it over the public address system to the whole school. Thanks to Barbara, by nine o'clock, every eighth grader in the school knew there was an animal in a basket in the office.

Buddy's dad sent a student to the office to get the basket shortly after the Pledge of Allegiance and the morning announcements were read. As the morning lessons progressed, several teachers stopped by Dave Sterner's room to ask for permission to take Little Bear to their classrooms to show him to their students.

By the beginning of the first lunch period, Little Bear had made several guest appearances throughout the building. Only Ms. Kingcaid, who seemed to be allergic to everything, said that the "creature," as she put it, was not welcome in her room. She was heard saying that teachers are in school to teach students, not to operate a zoo. (Many of the students think that Ms. Kingcaid is allergic to life itself.)

Meanwhile, Buddy's class had not heard the news. His classroom and the other sixth grades are on the second floor in the new part of the school building, far away from the office and other classrooms. The teachers who teach there call it the "Secret Tower." They're usually the last ones to learn news, unless the secretary announces it to the whole building.

One time when there was an early dismissal due to icy roads, the "Tower Teachers" hadn't known that the students were going home early until the first bus arrival was announced. Early-dismissal decisions and other schedule changes were not announced ahead of time because the kids tend to get a bit crazy when they know they are going home early. On this occasion, a note had been sent to the teachers, but the student taking the note around forgot to go to the second floor to alert the sixth-grade teachers.

Buddy was having a terrible day, and he couldn't concentrate on any of his schoolwork. He had no appetite during lunch, which his class ate in their classroom as a special reward for good behavior the previous month. After lunch Buddy felt even more distracted because his class was reading *The Indian in the Cupboard*. As he explained to his mom last night, one character in the book is an Indian named Little Bear.

The book is about a magic medicine cabinet. When a special key belonging to the main character's grandmother is used to lock the cabinet, the toys that are placed in it come alive. Even though Buddy loved the book, he wasn't able to pay attention. The day was taking forever to pass by. Every time he heard the name Little Bear mentioned, he became more upset. His thoughts continued to drift to playing with his own Little Bear.

Each student in the class had a paperback copy of the book. Classmates were taking turns reading aloud to the rest of the class. As he daydreamed about playing with the pup, Buddy became totally lost in his thoughts. He was dreaming about Mom and Dad giving him permission to keep his Little Bear, and he had no idea what was going on in class. The only words that registered in his cluttered brain were when someone read the words "Little Bear" while reading orally from the book. He was so lost in his own world that he didn't hear Mr. Cruise call his name to continue the oral reading.

"Buddy, will you please continue reading." Buddy was sitting in his seat with a blank stare on his face. He was gazing past the world globe out the window at an imaginary world of his own. He pictured Little Bear chasing him back and forth in his backyard. Mr. Cruise realized Buddy was daydreaming again. Daydreaming was one of Buddy's major problems in school.

"Mr. Buddy Sterner," Mr. Cruise called out in a loud voice, "I want you to read! Do you know what page we're on?"

Shocked back to reality by Mr. Cruise's loud and irritated voice, Buddy quickly shouted, "I don't know anything!"

Everyone began giggling, but Buddy did not see anything funny. Mr. Cruise was not amused either.

"Class, this is not an amusing situation. I do not want to hear any laughing."

The laughter made Buddy's day even more horrible. He was so embarrassed, he actually felt sick. He was about to raise his hand to ask for permission to go to see the nurse. Maybe the nurse, Mrs. Barthol, would send him home early, but that was doubtful because no one was at home that could take care of him. Perhaps he would be allowed to lie down for the rest of the afternoon in the health room. He really did have a stomachache. It was probably a combination of being embarrassed by his classmates laughing at him and wanting to go home to play with Little Bear.

As he put his hand in the air to ask permission to go to the nurse's office his dad entered the room carrying the pack basket. Dad placed the basket on Mr. Cruise's desk. As Buddy watched in delight, first one paw, then another, and finally Little Bear's head appeared at the top of the basket. It was just the medicine Buddy needed. His stomachache disappeared and he felt great. The pup's appearance in the classroom was like a miracle drug.

"Mr. Cruise, do you mind if I leave this basket and its contents in your room for the rest of the day?" The kids began calling out for Mr. Cruise to say yes. They didn't know that Mr. Sterner and Mr. Cruise had talked earlier about Little Bear coming to their classroom for the afternoon.

"Well, I don't know if my students would want to be bothered with a pup in a basket for the rest of the day," Mr. Cruise said with a big smile.

"Please, please let us keep him here!" The whole class shouted in unison.

"He has been in my class for a few hours and visited a few other classrooms, so I think he is ready for a change of atmosphere. However, if you really don't think you and your sixth graders want to be bothered, I'll take him back to my room," Dad answered, smiling back at Mr. Cruise.

"Well, I run a democratic classroom, so we will have to take a vote. Put your heads down and close your eyes. We will have a secret vote." Mr. Cruise and Buddy's dad always have their students vote with their heads cradled in their arms as if they were taking a nap. In that way, they are not tempted to vote the same way that their friends vote.

"Okay, raise your hand if you want Mr. Sterner to take this basket and its contents back to his room--and no peeking." Not a single hand was raised, but no one knew that except Mr. Cruise and Buddy's dad. "Okay, put your hands down. Now raise your hand if you want the pack basket to stay in our classroom for the rest of the day." Every hand went up.

"Wow, that sure is a close vote," Buddy's dad kidded.

"Yes, it looks like a tie to me. How will we break the tie?" As the two teachers talked, the students still had their heads down.

"Okay, raise your heads. It looks like we have a tie," Mr. Cruise teased, as the boys and girls looked at one another, wondering who voted to send the basket and the pup back to Mr. Sterner's room. Heads were shaking back and forth and shoulders were shrugged as students indicated they had not voted to send the pup away. "We have two choices. I can vote and break the tie or we can vote again." Not knowing how Mr. Cruise might vote, the class chose to revote.

"I'll tell you what. Let's vote again without putting your heads down. How many want Mr. Sterner to take the basket with him?" As before, no hands went up. "How many want the basket to stay here?" Every hand went up, including Buddy and a few of his friends who raised both hands. "Wow, from a tie to a unanimous decision. What are the chances of that many students changing their vote?" Both teachers smiled as the kids looked at each other with puzzled expressions on their faces.

"Well, I guess the pup has to stay with us!"

Every student applauded the decision.

Dad's eighth graders were in gym class, and he had five more minutes before he would meet his students in the gym. It was settled. The basket and its contents were going to stay in Mr. Cruise's room until it was time to go home. The most terrible day in school history was becoming possibly the best day Buddy had ever spent in school.

Buddy's Dad said goodbye and headed to the gym. Little Bear was whimpering in the basket. Mr. Cruise gave a short explanation of why the pup was in school and how Buddy had found him yesterday afternoon. The basket was still sitting on Mr. Cruise's desk. It practically tumbled over as the pup tried to climb out. Buddy sprang from his front row seat to Mr. Cruise's desk to steady the basket.

Everyone wanted to know every little detail about how Buddy saved the pup from a frigid night in the woods. Suddenly, Buddy was becoming the "Boy Hero" of Washington Middle School. Teachers' notes, delivered by student messengers, began arriving at Mr. Cruise's door. The notes requested that Buddy and the pup come to their classrooms to tell the story. Practically the whole school wanted to hear about the adventure at the Christmas tree farm.

CHAPTER SEVEN

A LOST PUP

The pup continued whimpering in the basket as Buddy told his classmates about the previous afternoon and why he had named the pup, Little Bear. Hoping to quiet the pup, Mr. Cruise decided to take him out of the basket, but first he placed Buddy's old blanket on the carpeted floor and surrounded it with four dark blue window-seat cushions that the students lie on while doing projects on the floor. He settled Little Bear in the middle, and in a short time, Little Bear drifted off to sleep. Buddy finished his story and was answering questions when Mr. Cruise announced that it was time for art class.

Unfortunately, all did not go well for the remainder of the afternoon. When Buddy's class went to Mrs. Eslinger's art room for their art lesson, Mr. Cruise walked to the copy room to run off worksheets and a test. While the copy machine warmed up, he returned to his room to check on the pup and to make sure the door was closed tightly.

The pup was asleep, nestled in the blanket behind the desk next to the wooden bookshelf where the classroom library books were stored. With the door closed, Little Bear would not be able to wander out of the room even if he awoke before Mr. Cruise and the students returned from art class.

During the time everyone was gone, Mr. Rothrock came into the classroom to check the thermostat. A new heating and cooling system had been installed last summer, and there were still problems in some classrooms. He left the classroom door slightly ajar as he adjusted the thermostat. Concentrating on his work, Mr. Rothrock did not notice Little Bear sneaking out through the open door. When Mr. Rothrock left the room, he closed the door tightly behind him.

The students and Mr. Cruise were very surprised to see that Little Bear was gone when they returned from their art lesson. Mr. Cruise assumed that someone, perhaps Buddy's dad, had come in and taken the pup back to his room, but just to be sure he called the office. Tears filled Buddy's eyes as Mr. Cruise made the call.

"Grace, this is Jim Cruise, will you please check to see if Dave Sterner or another teacher might have taken Dave's pup to their room?" Buddy felt a little better hearing Mr. Cruise refer to Little Bear as his dad's pup. Grace put through "an all-call," which is a way of contacting all the rooms at the same time.

No one responded that he or she had seen the pup. Buddy and the rest of the kids could not understand how Little Bear could open the door, close it again, and wander out on his own. Mr. Cruise told them how he had made a special trip back to the room to make sure the door was closed.

"I think he has magical powers!" Buddy called out with his hand waving high in the air, even though Mr. Cruise had not called on him. "He crawled out of the laundry sink last night even though my dad had put a heavy wooden tabletop and a barbell weight on the sink. He also escaped from a box I used to hide him in our garage. And I had put my dad's heavy tool chest on top of the box so he couldn't squeeze out."

"He's magical like the medicine cabinet in our book," Shirley chimed in. "I know he is!"

"Well I doubt that he has magical powers, but somehow he has disappeared," Mr. Cruise replied, reassuring the students that there was no magic involved.

At about three o'clock, as students and teachers were preparing for bus dismissals, an announcement came over the intercom to be on the alert for any glimpse of the missing pup. By that time the story had circulated through most of the building that Little Bear was missing from Mr. Cruise's sixth-grade classroom.

After hearing the announcement, Mr. Rothrock realized he had not closed the door to the room while he was working on the thermostat. He quickly went to Mr. Cruise and then to Dave Sterner's room to explain what had probably happened. He apologized for leaving the door open, but of course, he had had no idea Little Bear was sleeping on the floor behind Mr. Cruise's desk.

Buddy's Dad called Jim Cruise to explain what happened. "I know Dave, Rocky stopped here too."

Mr. Rothrock had to take care of his final chores before he went home and the night custodians arrived. Two of the three night custodians had arrived fifteen minutes early. After Mr. Rothrock explained the problem to them, the two night custodians joined him on a quick search for the pup before their work shift began. They decided to search the sixth-grade tower first because that was where Little Bear was last seen.

Buddy was very upset. "Mr. Cruise, may I please go to my dad's room to see if I can stay after school. If I stay later and go home with my dad instead of on the bus maybe we can find Little Bear."

"Okay, but hurry in case he says no and you have to go home on your bus. They will be announcing your bus any time now. Take your coat and backpack with you."

Buddy flew down the stairs, passing the NO RUNNING ON THE STAIRS! sign. Then he walked as fast as his eleven-year old legs could carry him without breaking the no-running-in-the-hall rule. He arrived in the eighth-grade section of the building before any buses were announced for boarding.

The door to his dad's room was closed. He could see Dad and his students reviewing the homework assignments. He knocked on the door and entered without waiting for someone to open it.

"Dad, can I go home with you today so I can stay and search for Little Bear?" he blurted out in a loud voice.

"I'm sorry Buddy, but I have a parent coming in for a conference in ten minutes and I must dismiss my bus students. You have to go home on your bus," he said. Then he asked Buddy to come to his desk and whispered, "I do not want you barging into my room without permission. I don't want other students thinking you have special privileges because you are my son. I know you are upset that Little Bear is missing. After my conference I will search the building and I am sure I will find him. Right now I need you to go home on the bus."

As Dad finished giving Buddy instructions, Grace called for Bus 7 students to be dismissed. Dad again reassured Buddy that he would look for Little Bear and bring the pup home as soon as the parent conference was over.

The bus ride seemed to take forever. Buddy and Chris discussed theories of where Little Bear might have gone. At home, Buddy paced back and forth through the house, anxiously waiting for a phone call or for Dad to come home. It was almost five o'clock. As Buddy passed the window for what seemed like the hundredth time, he spotted his dad's beige and brown van at the bottom of the driveway. Buddy flew out the door and raced down the driveway to meet him.

"Did you find him? Did you find him?" Buddy yelled. To his disappointment, Little Bear had not been found.

"No, the night custodians searched until they had to start their duties. Mr. Rothrock, Mr. Cruise, and I kept looking, but we didn't find him. I couldn't stay any longer. Mr. Cruise and I left together, but Mr. Rothrock continued searching. Maybe he will find the pup and call us."

When Mom arrived home, Buddy ran to tell her what had happened. His eyes filled with tears as he stammered, "Little Bear... disappeared... at school. Mr. Rothrock accidentally... left the door open... when he went in to check the thermostat in our room."

"Calm down, I can barely understand you!"

Buddy continued, "... and no one can find him. And Dad had a parent conference ... and I had to come home on the bus ... and he and the custodians looked ... and they didn't find him."

"That's terrible. The poor little thing, he's all alone in that big school with no one there to take care of him."

It was a sleepless night for the Sterners. Mom, Dad, and Buddy were still awake when the phone rang about midnight. Buddy ran to his parents' bedroom, hoping for good news.

Dad always answered the telephone in the same way. "Hello, this is the Sterner residence." It was Mr. Rothrock.

"Dave, this is Tom Rothrock, I'm sorry to bother you so late, but I stayed to look for Little Bear after you went home. The night crew had to get their work done. I knew they wouldn't have any time to search for the pup and after all, it was my fault that he wandered off. I knew you'd want to know what's up."

"You didn't need to do that! It's late and you should be home getting some rest and you have to open the building early tomorrow morning, but I am glad you called."

"Who is it? Did they find Little Bear?" Buddy interrupted.

"Please wait so I can find out. It's Mr. Rothrock and he's trying to tell me," Dad said, putting his hand over the telephone mouthpiece so Mr. Rothrock would not hear him talking to Buddy.

Mr. Rothrock continued his story. "I searched everywhere. I looked in the furnace room, the gym, and the storage closet. Then I searched every room a second time. I also thought he might have slipped outside, so I searched the playground area with a spotlight. Then the police arrived. A neighbor had called them to report that someone was wandering around the playground with a flashlight. Of course, it was me with my light! The two officers turned on the spotlights on the sides of their cars, but we didn't see Little Bear." Mr. Rothrock always tells every detail of a story.

Buddy was impatient. "Did they find him? Did they find him?" Buddy asked, standing on his parents' bed. Dad made a teacher frown and told him to settle down. Mom pulled Buddy down beside her on the edge of the bed and put her arm around him.

"Finally, I found Little Bear sleeping next to one of the bottom bookshelves in the corner cubicle of the library. You know what's really weird? He was lying next to a book titled Julie of the Wolves. Isn't that a crazy coincidence? The book was halfway off the shelf. Do you think it is some kind of mystical clue to what kind of animal he is? Do you think he might be a wolf pup? I gave him some small pieces of bread crusts soaked in milk. He was pretty hungry. He gobbled it right down."

"Oh, come on Dad, what's going on?" Buddy struggled out from under Mom's arm to stand beside the bed. He could not wait to find out what was going on.

"I doubt it, Tom," Dad answered, trying to hold a conversation and calm Buddy down at the same time.

"You doubt what?" Buddy questioned.

"I'll put the pup in a large box in the maintenance office until you come to school in the morning," Mr. Rothrock explained.

"The pack basket and blanket are still in my classroom. If it's not too much trouble, do you mind going to get the basket? Put the basket in the office?" Buddy did a little dance, having figured out from Dad's side of the conversation that Little Bear had been found. Why else would Dad tell Mr. Rothrock to go get the pack basket"?

"I'm on my cell phone. Do you want to wait while I go get the basket?" As he went to retrieve the basket with Little Bear under his arm, Mr. Rothrock continued telling more details of how he had carefully searched the building.

Dad nodded his head and smiled toward Buddy. He formed a circle using the end of his index finger and the end of his thumb indicating that Little Bear was found and was okay. "I'll tell you and your mom what happened in a minute. Mr. Rothrock is getting the basket from my room and he's explaining in detail what happened," Dad whispered. Dad's classroom was near the office, so Mr. Rothrock returned quickly.

Buddy leaped onto the bed and started jumping up and down like it was a trampoline. Mom was sitting next to him. She looked like she was riding a bucking bronco. "They found him, he's safe!" Buddy shouted as he bounced.

"I'm back in the office. The pup is safe in the basket. I will place Grace's large desk calendar on top of the basket and put a dictionary on top of the calendar. That way Little Bear will have air, but he will not be able to crawl out of the basket. He will be fine in the basket for the rest of the night."

"Thank you for all your help. Go home and get some sleep. You must be very tired. I will see you in the morning."

"Goodnight Dave."

"Goodnight Tom, and thanks again for all your trouble." Dad told Buddy and Mom the good news. He shortened the long story Mr. Rothrock had told him.

"Why don't we go get Little Bear right now?" Buddy cried out.

"Because the custodians have all gone home and the school is locked."

"Don't you have a key?"

"No, and the security alarms are set. You will have to wait until tomorrow morning."

"Yes, it's time to go to bed. We all have busy days ahead of us tomorrow," Mom added. "And this is the second night in a row that we are not getting enough rest.

Even though he didn't fall asleep until almost one o'clock, Buddy was awake before his alarm went off at six thirty. For one of the first times in his whole life, he couldn't wait to go to school. After a bit of begging, Dad agreed to take Buddy to school with him so Buddy could reunite with Little Bear before the hustle and bustle of the arriving school buses.

Buddy couldn't wait to see his little friend. Dad had barely applied the parking brake on the van when Buddy opened his seatbelt, threw open the passenger door, raced to the front entrance and bounded into the office. Little Bear was sitting on Grace's desk. She was working on the daily announcement sheet with one hand and petting the pup with the other hand. Mr. Rothrock was there, too. Buddy thanked him for finding the pup and taking good care of him.

Buddy was especially excited about the pup being in school for another day. It was a typical Tuesday, other than Buddy's several trips to teachers' rooms to show his furry friend and to tell the story about his Sunday afternoon tree farm adventure. Buddy was growing more and more attached to the pup.

The school day ended with Mr. Cruise reviewing assignments and explaining the Tuesday riddle. Every Tuesday, Mr. Cruise gave the class a riddle to figure out for homework.

Mr. Cruise explained, "There are three water glasses on a table. Two are full of water, but the third one is only half full." He drew a diagram of the three glasses on the chalkboard as he explained the riddle. "What famous king do these clues and diagram describe?"

Although Buddy had been distracted most of the day by Little Bear, he paid careful attention to Mr. Cruise's riddle. Buddy loved the riddles and always looked forward to the Tuesday riddle assignment. Even with the drawing as a clue, this riddle had him stumped, but Buddy thought that if he kept it in the back of his mind, perhaps he'd figure it out later. He quickly scribbled the drawing in his notebook.

CHAPTER EIGHT

THE GREAT PLAN

Mr. Cruise received a note from Buddy's dad at the end of the day. It contained instructions for Buddy.

Jim,

Do not send Buddy home on the bus. Keep him in your room until the buses leave and then send him to my room. I'm going to take him and the pup home with me. I'll notify Jerome, the bus driver, so he knows that Buddy won't be riding the bus.

Thanks,
Dave

Mr. Cruise called Buddy to his desk. "I have a note from your Dad. He wants you to go back to his room to go home with him today. He will tell the bus driver that you won't be on the bus."

Buddy was excited. Just think, he and Little Bear were going to ride home with Dad. It was another good sign. When Buddy arrived at Dad's classroom, his happy mood changed. Dad was making posters to place at the local businesses near where they live.

"We have to try to find Little Bear's owners. If this pup accidentally wandered off, I'm sure his owners are very upset. Help me finish the posters by putting our phone number on them using this permanent marker," Buddy felt like writing the phone number incorrectly.

On the way home, they placed posters at Marty's Market, the gas station, Jake's tree farm, and several other businesses in the area. By the time they arrived home, Mom had dinner on the table.

The family discussed the events of the day. Mom had gone shopping on her way home and bought puppy food and two small matching dog bowls for food and water. This was another sign the pup would be around for a while, but how long?

The placing of the posters had ruined Buddy's happy mood. Mom put a bowl of puppy food on the floor behind the kitchen table and added water to the water bowl. Little Bear dined along with the family. Later, Buddy played with the pup between attempts to complete his homework. Everyone finally had a restful night's sleep.

On Wednesday morning, Mom did not have to go to the hospital. She planned to catch up on housework and to keep Little Bear company. Buddy could sense that his Mom was growing quite fond of Little Bear, too. Dad was a different story. Buddy had to find a way to have Dad spend more time with the pup. The day at school passed very slowly, but Buddy was working on a plan.

Finally the bus dismissals were announced. It seemed like it took forever for Buddy's bus to reach his bus stop. Leaping to the ground from the bus, Buddy ran up the driveway as fast as he could go. He never heard Jerome yell at him for jumping out the door and not using the steps.

"How was school today?" Mom called. Buddy didn't answer. He was already on the way to his bedroom to change his clothes. "Now where did that boy get to already?" Mom thought, surprised that Buddy had not stopped to play with Little Bear. But Buddy had more important things to do. If his plan worked, he would have plenty of time to play with the pup.

Buddy emptied his book bag, quickly changed his clothes, grabbed his bike, and took off pedaling down the driveway. He had figured out a plan, a great plan: He would collect all the posters that he and Dad had placed at the local businesses last night.

Buddy didn't tell his mom where he was going. That was the first broken rule. He pedaled as fast as possible to Marty's Market, ran into the store, bought a candy bar so Chris's dad would not be suspicious, grabbed the poster pinned to the corkboard on his way out, and stuffed it into his empty book bag. Buddy put his arms through the straps of his book bag, threw it over his shoulders and was off pedaling his way to collect the next poster.

The next stop was the auto repair station. Buddy told a little white lie when Jack, the mechanic and owner, asked why he was removing the poster.

"Hey Buddy, how come you're taking the poster down? Did you find the owner already?" Jack asked.

"Yeah we found the owner!" Buddy yelled as he stuffed the poster in the bag and rode off on his bike. Buddy had been taught to be very honest, so he was upset with himself. It wasn't like him to break rules or lie to anyone. He thought about Mom's favorite saying. "Do unto others as you want others to do unto you," or something close to that. Was he breaking more rules?

As he rode toward the tree farm, Buddy convinced himself that he was the owner of the pup. "Hey, if I own the pup, then I didn't tell a lie to Jack. I did find the owner. It's me! Yes, I am the owner of Little Bear," Buddy said as threw both arms in the air and sat high on his seat just like the bike racers do when they cross the finish line at the end of a race. He quickly put both hands back on his handlebars as he approached Jake's dirt lane. A fall over the handlebars would ruin his great plan.

Sneaking into Jake's barn, Buddy grabbed the poster from the tree-farm bulletin board, stuffed it into the book bag with the others, and headed off again to retrieve the final three posters. He had to be home by dark. It was probably the first time in his life he had gone to the tree farm without stopping to talk to Jake. After grabbing the final poster at the garden center, he doubled back through the tree farm lane that wound up the hill toward his house.

Buddy ran into the house out of breath, threw his coat on the coat tree, and started playing with Little Bear. He had done it. He collected every poster and was home before dark.

Dad arrived home shortly after Buddy. "Elizabeth, I'm home," he called out. Mom met him in the kitchen. "You know what? I stopped at Marty's to pick up bread and milk and the poster wasn't on the news board."

"Maybe the real owners took the poster in order to call us about coming for the pup," Mom replied. Just then, Buddy entered the kitchen with a big smile on his face. His smile faded when he heard his parents' conversation.

"I replaced it with another poster I had in the van," Dad said. "I figured I better put up another one just in case the one we dropped off yesterday was thrown away or taken by someone."

Dinner was later than usual because Mom had run errands in the late afternoon. Buddy didn't say a word at the dinner table until Dad asked, "How was your day, Buddy?"

"Okay," he mumbled, thinking about how he could get rid of the new poster at the market. It was dark, so he could not go there on his bike.

"Just okay?"

"Yeah, just okay." Then it dawned on Buddy what to do! He hit himself on the forehead with the palm of his hand, wondering why he hadn't thought of it right away. "Mom, may I please be excused?"

"Yes, but put your dishes in the dishwasher first." Buddy stacked his plates, dropped his silverware in the tray and immediately called Chris. Chris was working on his homework when the phone rang. It was 7:30, and the market would close at 8:00. "Hello." Buddy recognized Chris's voice.

"Chris, listen carefully." Buddy quickly explained how he had ridden his bike to all the businesses and collected the posters. He continued, "My Dad stopped for milk and bread on the way home from school, and he put up another poster on your news board. Can you sneak down and remove it?"

"Wow, what a cool plan. Why didn't you tell me about collecting the posters?"

"I didn't have time at school and then I would have told you on the bus, but your mom picked you up at school to go to your trumpet lesson. Will you go get the poster? Go right now, before your Dad locks the doors."

"Sure, I'll go get it and I'll call you right back."

Five minutes later Buddy's phone rang. Dad was waiting for a call too, and he answered on the kitchen phone before Buddy could grab the one in the living room. In his usual way Dad said, "Hello, this is the Sterner residence."

Meanwhile Buddy picked up the phone and heard Chris talking to Dad. "Hi, Mr. Sterner. This is Chris. Can I talk to Buddy?"

"I don't know if you are able to talk or not. Do you want permission to talk to him or do you want to know if you know how to talk?" This was Buddy's dad's way of having kids correctly say may I instead of can I.

Chris just sighed and replied, "May I please talk to Buddy, Mr. Sterner?"

"That's better. Now I understand what you mean. Yes you may talk to Buddy. "Buddy," Dad yelled, "Chris is on the phone." Dad always enjoyed teasing Buddy's friends.

"Okay, Dad I have it!" Buddy yelled to Dad from the living room. He waited a bit until he was sure Dad was not still on the other phone. "Did you get it?" Buddy whispered.

"Yup, and I tore it into little pieces and ate the evidence just like in the spy movies."

"Get out! You didn't really eat it? Did you?"

"Nah, actually, I ripped it into a million little pieces and put them in the store's garbage can." Chris was prone to exaggerations.

"Great, I'll see you on the bus in the morning!"

Buddy slept well that night, knowing that for at least one more day, no one would be calling the number on the posters to claim Little Bear.

The plan worked. Dad never discovered that all the posters had disappeared, including the second one he tacked on the market bulletin board.

The rest of the week was uneventful. Saturday morning arrived crisp and clear. Buddy was very excited. His parents had decided to take the pup to the veterinary clinic in order to see if there had been any inquiries from customers about a lost puppy. They had a ten o'clock appointment. Also, they were hoping to find out whether the veterinarian could tell them what kind of dog Little Bear might be.

CHAPTER NINE

THE VET AND DOCTOR KENYON

Mom carefully strapped the pack basket to the back seat with the seat belt. The three Sterners and the pup headed to the vet. Buddy sat next to the basket to make sure that Little Bear did not climb out. Buddy constantly had to push Little Bear's small paws and head back into the basket as the pup continued to try to get out.

Amy, the young receptionist, made a big fuss over the pup. "What a cute pup. This is why I like this job. I get to see all the animals. I feel so good when they leave feeling better than when they came in. What can I do for you?" She rattled on without taking a breath or waiting for an answer. "What kind of a puppy is it?" It was about the fiftieth time that someone had asked that same question.

"That's one of the reasons why we're here. We're hoping the doctor will be able to tell us what he is," Buddy's dad explained. "Everyone at the school where I teach has their own theory." Dad told Amy a short version of the story about how Buddy found the pup almost a week ago. Dad also asked if anyone had stopped by or called about losing a pup.

"Well, no one to my knowledge has called in about losing a puppy, and after hearing the story, I want to know what he is too. I would be happy to adopt the pup if no one claims him or if you are not planning to keep him. He is so adorable! I'll page the doctor." She chattered on again, hardly stopping to breathe.

As Amy continued babbling on about this and that, the doctor came into the waiting room. "Hello, I'm Doctor Liana Irvine. Please bring the pup with you and follow me into the examination room."

The Sterners followed her into the examination room. Buddy carried the pack basket.

Dr. Irvine was an attractive, dark haired, slim woman, dressed in a light green knee-length medical robe. She was new at the clinic, which is the same clinic where Mom used to take her dog, Brandy.

The doctor extended her hand to greet Buddy, Mom, and Dad. "And who is this little guy?" she asked as she picked Little Bear out of the basket. He was running in midair, trying to get away from the doctor. "And what kind of dog is he?" she asked. There was that question again, number fifty-one out of a possible million more to come.

"That's what we were hoping you would tell us."

"I found him last Sunday in the weed field near Jake's Tree Farm. Do you know where that is?" Buddy asked.

"Yes, that's where my husband and I bought our Christmas tree. We just moved here on Thanksgiving weekend. It's a beautiful area. We lived in downtown Philadelphia before and…"

Buddy quickly interrupted the Christmas-tree-and-Philadelphia story asking whether the doctor could tell him what type of animal or dog Little Bear might be.

"Oh, so that's your name," she said to the pup as she checked his teeth. "You sure do look like a little bear."

Dad said, "The pup has a tail though, and bears do not have noticeable tails." Dad continued to point out to everyone about the tail.

"It's very hard to distinguish among dogs of the same breed, let alone those that are found as strays. For example, pedigreed cocker spaniels and beagles vary in their features and that's within the same breeds."

"Do you have any ideas?" Buddy prodded.

"No I'm sorry, but I do know that you have a very cute healthy little pup, and he is about five weeks old."

"How can you tell his age?"

"I can tell his age by the size of his teeth. From what you've told me, he is very lucky that a kind boy like you found him." Her comment brought a big smile to Buddy's face.

"I'm certain he would have died if you had not found him. It was unbelievably cold on Sunday night. I know, because I had to go out in the middle of the night to take care of a sick horse. It's great that your family has decided to adopt this little guy." Buddy beamed with joy as he intently listened to the doctor.

That's when Dad cut in again. "Well, that has not been decided. We are trying to locate the owners. Could we put a poster here? Perhaps the people who bring their pets here might recognize him."

"I'll tell you what, before you leave, I will have Amy take a digital photo of Little Bear, then print the photo and we'll put it on our bulletin board along with your poster."

"Oh great," Buddy thought. He did not want to have to sneak back to the clinic to retrieve another poster.

"Do you think he is a wild-animal baby?" Buddy asked, anxious to know what Little Bear's background might be.

"No, he probably wandered off from his owners, or perhaps he is the pup of a stray female. It is unusual for a stray female to have puppies outside in the winter like this, but it does happen. He seems to be too friendly and passive to be wild."

"Buddy found him on Sunday, and this is Saturday. You mean he was only four weeks old then?" Mom said as the doctor handed Little Bear to her.

"Yes, isn't it amazing? It's very unlikely that a four-week-old puppy could have made it through the night last Sunday. The cold weather we have been having leads me to doubt that he was out there longer than that one day. And puppies usually are not separated from their mother until they are about six to eight weeks old. He sure is lucky that your son found him."

"Doctor, we studied the circulatory system in school, and we talked about DNA tests. I was wondering if you might be able to take a DNA test to see what kind of animal Little Bear is."

"I'm sorry, but we do not have the equipment to do a DNA test. It's a rather complicated field of technology, and we normally would not have the supplies because in most cases we know the background of the puppies we treat because we also care for the puppy's mothers."

Buddy was noticeably upset when the doctor said that a DNA test was not a possibility.

"However, I do advise, for your protection and for Little Bear's welfare, that he receive puppy shots and a complete checkup as soon as possible. My next appointment cancelled this morning, so I have the time right now if you want me to check him thoroughly. Amy can get the shots ready, and you can bring in a stool sample on Monday or Tuesday so we can check him for worms."

Buddy knew that if his parents agreed to have the pup checked, the possibility of Little Bear joining the family was increasing. Mom and Dad huddled together and whispered back and forth.

He heard Mom say, "Well, Honey, we are here. Maybe we should save ourselves another trip and get it done now."

Buddy smiled a coy smile when he heard his Dad say, "No one has called about the pup even though we placed posters at most of the local businesses. And it will be a whole week tomorrow since he was found. What do you think, Buddy, should we save a trip and have the shots and checkup done now?"

Buddy didn't answer; he just ran to Dad and gave him a big hug. The pup's future in the Sterner home was looking very bright. Buddy was eager to go home and play with the pup. By the time Dr. Irvine had given the pup his shots and finished the general exam, Dad and Mom had forgotten about the poster and picture for the clinic bulletin board. But, Amy, even though she seemed like a bit of an airhead, stood there with the camera and reminded them about taking the photo of Little Bear.

Little Bear fell asleep in the pack basket before they reached the van. He was sleeping soundly as Mom strapped the basket onto the seat.

"Let's stop at the market and the other businesses to see if anyone has inquired about the posters," Dad said as they pulled out of the clinic lot on to Cherryville Lane. Realizing that none of the posters would be there, Buddy suddenly felt a terrible stomachache coming on. "Can we please go straight home?" he asked anxiously. "I think I might have to throw up." His parents gave him a funny look, but they drove straight home.

When they arrived home, Little Bear was still sleeping. Buddy had a miraculous recovery and felt fine. Mom had a project list ready for Dad to work on during the afternoon. When Buddy wanted to wake Little Bear to play Mom cautioned that the shots had probably made the pup drowsy and he should be allowed to continue with his nap in the basket.

So, Buddy grabbed his bike and headed down to Marty's Market to play with Chris. As they took turns on their bikes jumping a ramp that they had made with an old piece of one inch thick plywood and two cinder blocks, they talked about how Buddy removed the posters on Tuesday after school.

"You know, I feel bad about taking the posters down, but I just couldn't stand the thought of someone calling to claim Little Bear. I hope my Dad never finds out what I did. I believe that Little Bear wandered off from his mother and that is when I found him."

"Yeah, if your dad finds out what you did he might hang you on a tree using Little Bear's leash." Chris laughed, picturing Buddy running down the driveway with Mr. Sterner chasing after him swinging the leash like a rodeo rope.

That night Buddy kept the basket and the pup in his bedroom. Both of them had a peaceful night's sleep. Sunday passed quickly. When Buddy got up Monday morning, Dad told him it was snowing and school was delayed two hours. Dad planned to go in at the regular time in order to catch up on some papers he had not brought home to correct over the weekend. It was only one week until the third quarter report cards were scheduled to be sent home.

Buddy offered to go in early to help Dad. He also begged to take Little Bear to school again. Mom had to work at the hospital, so no one would be home with the pup.

Dad finally agreed. "Okay, I will call Pete to see if it is alright to bring your pup into school again."

"It's going to be a short schedule today with the late start, so I see no reason to leave Little Bear home alone," Mr. Pete responded.

Dad and Buddy hopped into the van and departed for school.

As they drove, Buddy struck up a conversation. "Dad, I have a riddle for you. What if there are three water glasses and two are filled, but the third one is only half full. What king does that remind you of?"

"That's an easy one. It's Phillip the third (Phillip III)."

"What does that mean?"

"You know, you have to fill up the third glass! King Phillip the third."

"Oh, now I get it!" Buddy said with a big grin.

"Hey, that's not one of the riddles that Jim Cruise gave your class to figure out, is it?" Buddy just grinned from ear to ear and said nothing, but Dad knew he had given Buddy the answer to the riddle.

Principal Peterson was busy in his office when they arrived at school. He was happy to see the pup and took him back to his office.

Mrs. Jones, the other secretary, had come in early too. She was excited that Little Bear was back at school. "I might not accomplish very much with the pup here," she joked. She was making copies of the report cards for the teachers that had turned them in early.

As before, Little Bear attracted a great deal of attention. Only Ms. Kingcaid was not overwhelmed by his presence. "School is for education; it is not an animal daycare facility," she grumbled. She always told everyone exactly how she felt about things.

The morning passed quickly. Students arrived at ten forty-five and classes started at eleven o'clock. Lunch periods started at eleven-thirty. The sixth grades had a special program scheduled right after the lunch periods were over. The lunchroom was a multi-purpose space, so special programs were held there, too.

Dr. Christine Kenyon, a world traveler and well-known photographer and author, was the speaker. Her program included a PowerPoint presentation of animal photos from her various photography trips. One photo showed a large snake swallowing a frog. The boys loved that one, but most of the girls made faces and grumbled in disgust.

When the program was over, the children were allowed to ask Dr. Kenyon questions. Buddy raised his hand. Dr. Kenyon called on him. "Do you think you can identify an animal I found about a week ago?" Buddy asked.

"I'll do my best. Do you have a photo?"

"I don't have a photo; he's here in the office." Buddy was given permission to go to the office and bring back Little Bear while Dr. Kenyon answered more questions. By the time Buddy brought Little Bear back to the all-purpose room, the students were exiting to their classrooms.

Buddy excitedly asked Dr. Kenyon if she could tell what type of animal Little Bear might be.

"You can call me Dr. Chris. That's what my good friends call me." Buddy beamed at the invitation to call this famous woman by the name her friends used. She examined the pup very carefully. Like everyone else, she thought Little Bear was adorable. Unfortunately, she was not able to determine what kind of animal he was, but she was sure Little Bear was not a wild animal. "He's too docile to be wild."

"Would you please excuse me?" Buddy was being very polite. He ran over to Mr. Cruise as his class was leaving the room. "Mr. Cruise, may I please have permission to stay a couple of minutes to ask Dr. Chris more questions?"

"Dr. Chris? Her name is Dr. Kenyon!

"I know, but she said I could call her Dr. Chris."

"Okay, you may stay for a couple more minutes, but you must be back in our classroom by two o'clock. Our sixth-grade schedule was adjusted because of the late start, and you must be in line at Ms. Kingcaid's room for language arts on time. You have about ten minutes. I mean it; don't be late for language arts class."

Buddy quickly ran over to Dr. Chris and told her his story about finding Little Bear. She thought it was a great story and suggested that it would be a wonderful basis for writing a book for children. She suggested, "You should write down all the details. We soon forget many of the things we experience during our lives." She encouraged him to jot down everything and put it in a safe place. "Maybe someday, you will want to write your story."

"But I hate to write."

"I also hated to write when I was young, but now I'm the author of several books based on my travels," she responded. "You never know what you might do with your education someday." She had also published two books of her photographs. Buddy helped her carry her lecture equipment to her car.

After she finished packing her materials into the trunk of the car, Dr. Kenyon did something that surprised Buddy. She took out a copy of her most recent photography book on animals of the United States. Opening the cover, she wrote, "To Buddy, an inquisitive young man. Someday I hope to read the full story about Little Bear." Then she signed her name. Buddy thanked her, said good-bye, and ran to his classroom. He had one minute left before language arts class would begin.

CHAPTER TEN

SUMMER FUN

The rest of the school year passed quickly for Buddy and his friends. The last day of school had come. It was June 15, the first day of summer vacation; a summer that would prove to be filled with fun. Buddy and his friends were playing in the front yard in his dad's rowboat, pretending to be sailing away from school, with the purpose of never returning to school again. They were singing, "No more school, and no more books. No more teachers' dirty looks." Gene added, "Especially Ms. Kingcaid's dirty looks!" The boys laughed and sang the song over and over, making up their own verses.

Yes, summer had finally arrived. No more homework, tests, or reading assignments to worry about until September. Mom would have only two weeks of vacation time, though, and she envied Buddy and Dad, who had the full summer ahead of them. Dad joked that the three best things about being a teacher were June, July, and August. Mom did not think that Dad was very funny.

Buddy was excited because the family would be traveling to New York State for several days to visit Dad's college roommate and his family. After that, Mom and Dad told Buddy, they were planning to relax for a few days and then perhaps go on a few day trips or an overnight trip.

Little Bear was almost five months old, and he was about to go on his first big trip. Dad's college roommate, Rob, and his wife, Mary, own and manage a ski area near the border of Pennsylvania and New York.

Although they're not really related, Buddy calls them Uncle Rob and Aunt Mary, and their kids call Buddy's parents Aunt Elizabeth and Uncle Dave. Uncle Rob and Aunt Mary are Buddy's godparents. And Buddy's parents, in turn, are the godparents of Rob and Mary's oldest son, fourteen-year-old Tab. Rob and Mary also have a son Todd, who is the same age as Buddy. Toni, their daughter, is nine.

Buddy fashioned a travel platform out of plywood for Little Bear and had stapled an old piece of carpet around the plywood for padding. The platform rested on the seat behind Dad's seat in the van. A large picnic cooler doubled as a support for the platform and a place to keep snacks and drinks cold. It provided a great doggie seat and bed where Little Bear could sit up and look out the window or lie down and snooze.

Buddy and his parents discovered something new about Little Bear during the trip to New York. The family had traveled about forty-five minutes when Little Bear woke up and began to make strange noises. The noises sounded like "miu, miu, miu." Before Dad could pull the car to the side of the road, Little Bear moved forward on the platform. Unfortunately for Dad, the pup threw up all over the back of Dad's seat, on his neck, and down the back of his T-shirt.

"What in the world is that? " When Dad realized he had barf down his back he cried out, "I knew it, I knew it, I knew it! I should never have allowed you to keep that mutt!" Continuing to moan and grumble as he steered the car onto the shoulder of the road, Dad continued his tirade, "I don't believe it, I just don't believe it! I don't believe it!" He kept repeating the phrase as he set the emergency brake and turned on the emergency flashers. Poor Little Bear was feeling much worse than Dad was feeling at that point.

"Don't worry, Buddy and I will clean the seat, and I have extra clothes you can change into. I will wash your barfy clothes when we get to Rob and Mary's place," Mom calmly replied. "Stop at the next rest area." Mom and Buddy began to giggle, even though they knew they really shouldn't. It was much like when you find something to be funny in church or another quiet place and you know you should not laugh because everyone will hear you. The more they tried to stop, the more they laughed. Dad was not amused and grew angrier as Buddy and Mom continued giggling.

"It's not funny. How would you like barf all over you?"

"Oh, don't make such a big deal out of it. When Buddy was a baby, he often threw up on me. And don't forget how you always had some excuse to get out of changing his diapers," Mom uttered as she reached over to wipe some of the barf off Dad's neck with a tissue. Buddy was humming loudly. He didn't want to hear stories about when he was wearing diapers.

Dad knew he had lost the argument. Just as he was ready to pull safely back onto the highway, a state trooper pulled in behind them with roof lights flashing on his vehicle.

The trooper put on his hat as he approached their van.

"What's the trouble here, sir?"

"Well, actually, my son's puppy got carsick and we pulled over to take care of it. It landed on my neck and down my back," Dad complained. "I pulled over quickly to the side of the highway. We are safe and sound, sir."

"Well, I'm glad it's nothing that will delay your trip. Drive safely!" The trooper walked away with a big smile on his face.

"I don't know what he's smiling about," Dad grumbled as Buddy and Mom began giggling again.

Dad carefully pulled back onto the four-lane highway to drive the seventeen barf-covered miles to the next rest area, where they could properly clean up Little Bear's mess. Dad pulled into the rest area and cautiously backed into a parking spot. Mom began unpacking a clean shirt and shorts from the suitcase. Buddy put the leash on Little Bear and they jumped out of the side door and walked to the pet area. The pup ate some grass, "watered" a bush, and barked at a big truck. He seemed to feel much better being out of the van.

While his dad was changing into clean clothing Buddy spotted a maintenance man spraying the flowers with a hose and asked if he might be able to use the hose to spray water on Little Bear. The man obliged and Little Bear tried to bite the stream of water as it came from the hose. By this time Mom had brought an old rag towel to dry the pup off before they continued their trip.

The fresh air, exercise, and the spray from the hose all helped to calm the pup's stomach. After washing and changing in the men's room, Dad was in a better mood, too. Mom finished the unpleasant job of scrubbing the seat and other dirty areas with window cleaner. With a clean Dad, a clean seat, a clean floor, and a clean Little Bear, they continued on their way.

Dad was feeling good; in fact he was singing one of his shower songs when it happened again. They had traveled about fifteen miles when Little Bear began to make the same noises, "mui, mui, mui," and then the poor pup let go for the second time. Hearing the all-too-familiar sounds, Dad lunged forward in his seat, still managing to keep the van safely under control. Luckily, this time the mess missed Dad. It covered the platform, the back of Dad's seat, Little Bear and the carpeted van floor.

"He hardly ate his breakfast. I think he knew we were going away and he was worried that he would be left behind. I don't know where all the barf is coming from," Buddy said in the pup's defense.

Dad pulled the car into the next rest area and took a short walk to regain his patience. Mom and Buddy cleaned the platform and the van floor with more window cleaner. Giggling while they worked, Mom added the finishing touches by spraying a tiny bit of her perfume on the carpet.

Buddy took Little Bear for a quick flower-watering walk and some more fresh air. They returned to the van at the same time as Dad. Everyone got back in the van and fastened their seatbelts. The odor in the van wasn't the most pleasant odor, but it was much better than "Scents de Doggie Barf."

Dad was not in any mood to stop again. "I don't want to stop again until I pull into the ski area parking lot." He liked to drive straight through to the final destination whenever they went on vacation. Little Bear finally felt better and went back to sleep.

They hadn't traveled very far when Buddy whispered something to Mom.

"Honey, will you please stop at the next rest area so I may use the bathroom?" Mom said in a pleasant voice. She knew Dad would agree to stop if she said she needed to use the restroom. And while she really did need to stop again--having already drunk two glasses of homemade ice tea from the drink cooler--the stop was mainly for Buddy. Dad made a grunting noise, which may have meant yes.

"I will stop at the next rest area, but that better be the last time." Dad had hardly applied the emergency brake when Buddy took off his seat belt, threw open the side doors, and bolted for the restrooms. It was reminiscent of his exit the morning at school when Little Bear had been lost. Mom followed calmly, walking with the pup on his leash. When Buddy came out, he took Little Bear, so Mom could use the restroom.

The usual 150-mile, under 3-hour trip took 4 1/2 hours, including the four rest stops. Dad continued mumbling under his breath during the final miles of the trip.

This was the family's first visit to the ski area. Uncle Rob, Aunt Mary, and their children live in a cottage beside the top edge of the expert trail. Tab, Todd, and Toni ran toward the van as Dad pulled into the parking lot. They had been watching for the van from the ski lodge deck. After a set of quick hellos, the kids grabbed luggage and food bags from the van and began carrying them to the lodge.

Lightning, their new pup, was barking on the deck in front of the lodge. Little Bear ran up the steps where the pups sniffed one another for several minutes, and then they romped off toward the ski lift. The eight-foot-high security fence that enclosed the entire ski area made it a safe place for the pups to play. They began racing up and down the maintenance road with a trail of dust flying behind them. The pups were out of sight before the van was half unloaded.

By the time the four kids caught up with the dogs, the pups were frolicking and splashing through a small ditch and small pools that had formed from a rainstorm. Little Bear ran to each pool, lay down in the water, blew bubbles, and drank the water. Lightning ran around and around, splashing Little Bear with water, sand, and mud.

Both Lightning and Little Bear resembled mud-covered drowned rats as they trotted down the dry, dusty trail, following the kids toward the lodge. The dust coated their wet, muddy coats with another layer of dirt.

"You kids better wash those dogs before you bring them into the lodge," Uncle Rob yelled.

"We will, don't worry. You won't even know they were muddy," Tab yelled back.

"Yeah, Uncle Rob, you won't recognize them when we're done," Buddy added as the boys walked to the maintenance shed. Tab turned on the hose attached to the shed. They began rinsing the pups with cold well water. Toni arrived with some dog shampoo. When she went to pour a little bit of shampoo on Little Bear the cap fell off and half of the bottle of shampoo dropped onto the Little Bear's back. Toni quickly scooped up as much of the shampoo as she could and rubbed it on Lightning's back. It took plenty of water to wash off the mud from the pups' long fur and even more water to rinse all the extra shampoo from their coats.

"Toni, will you go for some clean towels? There's a bunch in a big cardboard box in the tool shed," Tab said to Toni, who was watching the two boys struggling with the pups.

"What am I, your gopher? Get it? You asked me to 'go for' towels."

"Yeah, yeah, I get it, so now you better get it. 'It' being the towels and you better get them right now or you might also accidentally become covered with water and shampoo."

"Can you say pretty please?" Toni shouted as she ran toward the shed for the towels. Tab tried to spray her with the hose as she ran off.

"You are so lucky, Buddy."

"Why?"

"You are lucky because you don't have a pain-in-the-neck little sister constantly driving you crazy!" Tab groaned.

The boys continued rinsing the pups. After grabbing a bunch of clean towels from the tool shed, Toni returned to the boys' puppy-style beauty salon. She held Little Bear by the collar while Buddy tried to dry him with one of the towels. Todd arrived with an old hair dryer and an extension cord. The pups continually pulled at their leashes, shaking, and spraying water on the four groomers.

"Lightning often comes home dirty, but this time he is really a mess," Tab said, rubbing Lightning with one of the biggest towels.

"Well, he had lots of help. I've never seen Little Bear this filthy either," Buddy laughed, as he continued drying his pup by hand. Todd was using the old hair dryer to help dry Lightning's fur.

Finally, the two pups, three boys, and Toni were clean and dry. Uncle Rob checked the dogs thoroughly before he allowed them to enter the lodge.

Uncle Rob and his family eat most of their meals in the lodge. Their meals are cooked and served by Marie, the ski-lodge cook, who also manages the lodge snack bar and restaurant. She works all year round making great meals for the family and the customers.

"It looks to me like you're getting a bit wider from all the good food Marie cooks," Dad said, poking fun at Uncle Rob. As usual Uncle Rob pretended not to hear the teasing comments.

The adults sat down to have a cup of coffee and to chat while the kids tried out the new trampoline. Aunt Mary had a strict list of trampoline rules including no wearing shoes while bouncing and only two bouncers at a time. The new trampoline had safety netting surrounding it to catch anyone who jumped off center too much.

"Hey Todd, nice socks" cried Tab and Buddy in unison. "They look great with your shorts and white sneakers," Tab said, bouncing on his knees. Todd was wearing a pair of black socks with white sneakers. Tab and Buddy continued bouncing while Todd was patiently timing them with his new stopwatch.

"It's my turn," he yelled after about ten minutes. As he took his sneakers off to take his turn bouncing, his two big toes poked through the large holes in both black socks. Buddy and Tab laughed hysterically. Todd wasn't worried about what he was wearing. He just wanted to jump and have fun on the trampoline. Jumping alone, he ignored the two boys as they continued to tease him about his socks. He pretended not to hear the teasing, knowing that if he argued back, he would not win. Todd was smart enough to realize you never win when it's two against one, and you happen to be the one.

Then, while Todd was doing a front flip, his left sock flew off. It sailed over the netting and landed on Lightning's head. Tab and Buddy rolled on the ground, laughing at the flying sock while the pup grabbed the sock and ran off with it in his mouth.

Soon Toni joined the boys. Little Bear had followed her from the lodge and Lightening had returned without Todd's holy sock in his mouth. The boys placed the pups on the trampoline and everyone took turns bouncing until they heard the bell that Marie rings to signal that meals are being served.

"Great, I'm hungry," cried Tab. "Last one to the lodge is a rotten egg!"

When they arrived at the lodge they found Buddy's mom ringing the bell. "Your mom wants the three of you to go wash up, and she wants you to help her with some shopping. You're supposed to meet her as soon as possible in the lodge kitchen."

"Can I go with them to town?" Buddy asked.

"No, Marie is cooking a late dinner and we're all going to eat together when Aunt Mary and the kids come back from shopping. You, Dad, Little Bear and I are going to take a walk before it gets dark."

It was about an hour before sunset when Little Bear, Buddy, and his parents left the lodge. Arriving at the summit, they climbed to the top of the steep ski ramp in order to get a better view of the surrounding countryside.

"It sure is beautiful and peaceful up here. Look at the gorgeous colors of the sky tonight." As Mom spoke, Little Bear found out the hard way that the front of the ramp facing down the mountain was steep and slippery.

Before he could turn around, he started to slide. For a couple of seconds, he appeared to be running on a treadmill. He was not gaining any ground as he tried to reach the level area of the ramp. Before anyone could help him, he landed in the safety net and then like a tuna trying to escape from a fishing net, he struggled, but finally fell through the crisscross ropes to the ground. It was about a ten-foot drop from the net to the ground. The pup landed safely and he was back on the ramp, looking for someone to pet him, before anyone had time to run down to see if he was okay.

"I don't think this pup feels any pain!" Mom commented.

The sun was beginning to set behind the distant hill as the Sterners and Little Bear hiked back down the maintenance road to the ski lodge.

CHAPTER ELEVEN

OLD STORIES

Marie prepared a fine dinner of fresh ham, baby carrots, mashed potatoes, gravy, and strawberry shortcake. After the great dinner, the kids begged Buddy's dad and Uncle Rob to tell stories about when they were in college. They loved to hear their fathers' crazy college stories. Even though they had heard the stories many times, they always wanted to listen to them again--especially when doing so allowed them to stay up past their normal bedtime.

"I finished my work in the kitchen. I will see you in the morning," Marie called to the group. She and her husband, Jerry, walked through the lodge on the way to the door. Jerry also works at the lodge, helping Uncle Rob with the chores and other projects.

"Why don't you sit and relax and listen to the guys' crazy stories about college," Aunt Mary suggested.

"Oh, if I sit down and relax I won't want to get up to go home, and if Jerry sits down he will probably fall asleep and no one will be able to wake him."

"Well, drive safely. You don't have to come in early tomorrow," Uncle Rob added. "It's Saturday. Get some rest."

"I'll be here by seven. I have a lot to do!" Marie said as she and Jerry said good-bye.

"Tell the story about Disneyland, Snow White and the dwarfs," Toni urged.

"You've heard that one at least a hundred times."

"But it always makes us laugh," the kids agreed.

"Okay, one more time, but I plan to shorten it," Uncle Rob finally agreed. "As you all know, Dave, our college friends Louie and Denny and I took a trip out west the summer before we all started working. And as you also know we went to most of the national parks and eventually to Disneyland. We had gone on several rides, and we were walking through Fantasyland. It was about noon when we decided to eat some lunch. Denny started talking to the young girl dressed as Snow White. Uncle Dave, Louie, and I also chatted with her about her job and how she liked working at Disneyland. She seemed about our age and she was very pretty and friendly.

"While we were talking to her, two Disneyland employees dressed in dwarf costumes approached us. I remember the one was Dopey, but I'm not sure which dwarf the other one might have been."

"I bet it was Bashful, that's why you don't remember which dwarf it was," Toni chimed in. "He was so bashful that you don't remember him."

"Do you want me to finish the story?" Uncle Rob stressed. "It's getting late. I think you kids should go to bed!"

"No, please finish the story!" Toni quickly responded.

"Okay, but no more interruptions!" Uncle Rob winked at Toni as he continued the story. "Yes, let's say it was Bashful and Dopey who approached us and as they came closer they were turning their bodies from side to side, causing their empty costume arms to swing back and forth across their bodies. They stopped walking when they reached Snow White and the four of us, but Dopey continued swinging his arms.

"His real arms were inside the costume along the sides of his body. He began swinging his arms in our direction. The swinging of the fake arms caused the heavy rubber hands to sting when they struck against us. We told him to stop, but he continued to swing his arms. Finally, Denny lost his temper when one of Dopey's rubber hands hit him squarely on his back. Denny whirled around, grabbed Dopey's fake arms and wrapped them around Dopey's real arms, which were hanging at his side in the costume. Dopey couldn't move.

"Denny told Dopey that he would let him go if he stopped swinging his arms and hitting us with the hard rubber hands. If not, Denny said, he was going to do more than just wrap him up in his costume arms. Dopey responded that Denny better let him go immediately or else. 'Or else what?' Denny asked. "Then, what Dopey said is something that none of us will ever forget."

The kids called out Dopey's words before Uncle Rob could say them. "You know, there are seven of us and there are only four of you," the kids shouted laughing so hard that their bellies ached.

"When Dopey yelled that there were seven of them, Dave, Louie, and I broke out laughing so hard and so long that we had side stickers. It sounded so funny. Even Snow White was laughing.

Denny replied, yes, there are four of us, but we aren't wearing stupid clumsy dwarf costumes."

Buddy's dad chimed in. "Denny was so angry, I don't think he even heard what Dopey said. I was worried that if Denny did anything to Dopey, the park security police might come and arrest all of us. I pictured calling my dad to tell him I was in jail for fighting with the Seven Dwarfs in Disneyland. Thankfully Dopey agreed and Denny released him. When Denny let him go the two dwarfs quickly walked away. We apologized to Snow White and invited her to have lunch with us."

Todd, usually the craziest of the four kids, quickly yelled out, "It would have been funny if the two dwarfs returned with the other five dwarfs and you all rolled around on the ground fighting," Todd said, laughing and rolling on the floor like he was in a fight with the dwarfs. "Take that, Dopey. Hey Sleepy, wake up and fight. Where did Bashful get too? Who just sneezed on me? What are you smiling about, Happy? Wipe that frown off your face, Grumpy. If I get a hold of you everyone will need Doc!" Everyone laughed at Todd's antics and no one could believe that he could name all seven dwarfs while he rolled around on the floor pretending to be fighting.

"What do you think Pappy would have done if you were arrested?" Buddy asked.

"I don't even want to think about that," Dad replied quickly. "You know how strict your Pappy can be, I doubt if he would have sent me any bail money. I would probably still be in jail!"

Buddy pictured Dad in a striped jail suit looking out from behind bars. He started laughing again. "Mom and I would come to visit you every year. It would have been funny if they had locked you up in Frontierland," Buddy added.

Dad continued, "I was about to start my first teaching job when we returned home from the trip. I pictured my photo on the front page of the local newspapers with the headline: 'New Cherryville School District teacher arrested for fighting with the Seven Dwarfs in Disneyland.' Then I imagined being fired by the school board before I started my first day as a teacher."

That is when Aunt Mary interrupted the stories, "Okay kids, it's time to go to bed".

"But we want to hear the story about Dad and Uncle Dave when they went to Mount Rushmore and pretended to be ripped off because they thought the president's faces were naturally formed by erosion not carved in the mountain," Toni begged.

"That is the whole story. You'll have to wait to hear all the details some other time. Now get up to the loft and go to bed."

The kids had sleeping bags for sleeping in the loft of the ski lodge. At least they were supposed to sleep. But when they were snuggled in their sleeping bags, the boys began teasing Toni about the time she had fallen asleep at the table.

About six years ago, well before they started running the ski area, Aunt Mary had been keeping dinner warm because Buddy and his parents were coming to visit. Aunt Mary wanted everyone to eat together, but dinner was delayed because Buddy and his parents had been stuck in traffic due to a tractor trailer accident. It wasn't as bad as this puppy-barf trip, but Dad had lost his patience sitting waiting for the accident to be cleared. When they finally arrived and dinner was served, Toni was asleep on the sofa. She had begged Aunt Mary to wake her so she could eat when everyone else was eating.

Aunt Mary did wake Toni so she could join the group at the table. Toni ate a few forks full of spaghetti when all of a sudden her head dropped; she fell back to sleep and her face landed in the plate of spaghetti and sauce. Aunt Mary quickly pulled Toni's head up. Noodles were hanging from her eyebrows and her nose. Her face was red with sauce. She was out cold, like a boxer lying in the ring after a knockout.

"I was only three years old and I was very tired. Aren't you ever going to let me forget that night?" Toni pleaded.

"No way," the three boys said at the same time.

"You'll be one hundred years old and we will still tell people about your famous spaghetti dive," Todd teased. Todd had such a great memory that he began retelling all the details of the story. Toni groaned and pulled her sleeping bag over her head. She was humming to herself and holding her hands over her ears, trying not to hear Todd's story of the incident.

"Hardly anyone lives to be a hundred years old anyway, and if I am one hundred, you'll be about one hundred and two," she yelled from deep within her sleeping bag. Todd continued the story, describing every detail, right down to the number of spaghetti noodles that had hung from the end of her nose and eyebrows. Finally the stories and giggling stopped as the tired indoor campers drifted off to sleep. Before they knew it, it was Saturday morning.

Everyone got up early. By seven forty-five, they were all seated at one of the lodge tables, enjoying one of Marie's great breakfasts. It was like a restaurant buffet. Marie cooked everything you could possibly have for breakfast. The boys loved to eat, and there was certainly plenty of food. After breakfast, Mom went hiking with the kids and the two pups. Buddy's Dad helped Uncle Rob and Jerry with some maintenance projects while Aunt Mary worked in the ski office.

The two pups led the way, as the hikers were heading to several small beaver ponds on the plateau about a half-mile beyond the top of the ski lift where Little Bear had performed his ski ramp dive the previous night. Frogs and turtles live in the pond and deer often come to the pond's shoreline to drink. Buddy and his Mom hoped to see the beavers. They had never seen beavers anywhere except in a zoo. Both pups disappeared into the woods as the hikers trudged up the side of the beginner's ski trail. A flock of wild turkeys came running out onto the trail with the dogs in close pursuit. The dogs chased the turkeys until the big birds flew up over the hill in the direction of the ponds.

When Mom and the kids reached the small ponds below the waterfall, the two pups splashed and chased each other along the shoreline. Lightening disappeared for a moment behind the beaver dam. The pup came back immediately when Tab whistled, but Lightning was carrying something in his mouth.

"Oh no," Mom screamed as Lightening approached. "He's carrying a rotting rabbit in his mouth. Drop that, drop it!" Mom screamed.

Then Little Bear grabbed the rabbit and the two pups started a tug of war with the decaying, stinky rabbit. Before anyone could do anything they both rolled on top of the rabbit like dogs often do when someone gives them a biscuit. Mom and the kids were repulsed by the terrible smell. Both pups needed a bath, but no one wanted any part of cleaning them. The five weary travelers trudged back to the lodge with the stinky pups following them.

This time Uncle Rob got stuck taking care of the pup problem. He had to take a break from his work to transport the smelly pups to the local dog grooming shop. He safely tied them in the back of the old pickup truck. Luckily, Lightening's grooming shop was only a half mile away. The stench from the rabbit was so bad that the groomer charged double to clean the pups.

When Uncle Rob went back to pick up the pups, old Hank told him he'd been grooming dogs for thirty-eight years and that he "ain't never seen or smelled two more stinkin' dogs then those two." Hank said it was even worse than when customers brought in dogs that had met up with the rear end of a skunk.

Hank did a great job and the pups came back looking like they were ready for a beauty contest. They smelled and looked wonderful.

"These pups look beautiful. Look, Old Hank even tied a ribbon on their collars," Aunt Mary commented admiringly.

"I don't know if you noticed, but I had to buy two new collars, too. Hank said he will soak the old ones, and we can have them back if the stench ever disappears."

Unfortunately, it wasn't very long before Little Bear was in trouble again. He ran over to the table and grabbed Uncle Rob's cheeseburger from his plate. Uncle Rob had just added all the condiments to the cheeseburger including lettuce, a fresh slice of homegrown tomato and onion. He was talking to Marie and didn't see what happened until everyone started laughing. Tired from the morning chores and his two trips to Old Hank's Grooming Palace, Uncle Rob was certainly in no mood to deal with the dogs again. Everyone thought it was funny, except Uncle Rob.

"I work all morning, I put up with two trips to the groomer through bumper-to-bumper traffic with two stinking mutts, and now this! What next?" What happened next happened very quickly. Lightning came up behind Uncle Rob from the other side and took the hot dog and roll from the plate while Uncle Rob was still complaining about losing his cheeseburger. With the second theft, everyone in the lodge had a good laugh. Even Uncle Rob had to smile, knowing he had been robbed twice.

"Don't worry, there is plenty more food," Marie said with a laugh as she headed to the kitchen for another tray of hamburgers and hot dogs. "Let those two pretty puppies enjoy their lunch," she called back as she pushed through the swinging doors into the kitchen.

"You mean let them enjoy *my* lunch, don't you?" Uncle Rob yelled back to Marie, as he began adding catsup and onions to the last cheeseburger on the original serving tray.

After lunch the boys went horseback riding on the ski trails. Buddy was not used to riding. He had only been riding once before and that was during a trail ride where each horse walked slowly in a single line.

"I always seem to be coming down as the horse and saddle are coming up." Buddy yelled out as he winced in pain. "My butt is sore and I think my teeth are shorter," he kidded.

"I don't know what you're complaining about," Todd yelled, galloping by with his right arm in the air like a rodeo rider. "It's so easy!"

"Yeah, you ride all the time, no wonder you think it's easy," Buddy yelled back, having trouble getting out the words as he continued bouncing up and down. He felt like he was bouncing higher than he had bounced on the trampoline the previous afternoon.

Tab, Todd, and Toni are good riders, but they have the opportunity to ride whenever they wish. Uncle Rob grew up riding and started teaching the kids to ride when they were very young.

After the boys brushed and rubbed down the horses, both families went to the lake located across the road from the ski area. Buddy's dad finally convinced Uncle Rob to take a break from his work schedule to join the others at the beach.

The boys swam out to the raft and began doing cannonballs into the water. Lightning and Little Bear splashed around in the shallow water near the shore. The adults relaxed on beach chairs, enjoying the afternoon sun. When the pups finally came out of the water they ran directly to where Buddy's dad was sitting. He was relaxing and sipping an ice tea while reading the sports section of the newspaper. Little Bear stopped on one side of Buddy's dad and Lightning stopped on the other side. Then as both pups began shaking the water from their bodies Dave Sterner was the unappreciative recipient of a surprise shower.

"Why did you come to me?" Buddy's dad shouted to the pups, trying to keep somewhat dry by using the newspaper as a shield. "Go over to the others and shake," he moaned, motioning toward Elizabeth, Mary and Rob sitting across from him.

"I guess you are just lucky," Uncle Rob teased. "At least they didn't steal your lunch."

The kids dried off the wet pups, and then everyone walked together back to the lodge. Marie prepared another wonderful meal. Uncle Rob took no chances this time. He made the pups stay outside on the deck in the front of the ski lodge during dinner.

It was soon time for bed. Buddy's dad decided to sleep in the loft with the kids so they would sleep and not talk all night long.

Lightning has a bad habit that no one had explained to Buddy and his parents. If the pup has the opportunity, he likes to drink out of the toilet. Uncle Rob, Aunt Mary, and the kids always put the toilet lids down so Lightning can't get a drink. Since, Buddy did not know about Lightning's preference for toilet water he did not put the toilet lid down when he used the bathroom at the end of the hall next to the loft. In the middle of the night, Lightning woke Buddy's dad with a big, wet toilet kiss.

"What in the world is that?" he cried out, as Lightning stood dripping above his face. Toni screamed, not knowing why Uncle Dave was yelling. Her scream startled the three boys, who sat straight up in their sleeping bags yelling louder than Toni because they did not know what was happening. When they realized why Buddy's dad was yelling they began laughing. They stopped quickly when they noticed the grim look on Uncle Dave's face. The kids each crawled back into their own sleeping bag to finish giggling.

"Tab, will you please take your dog somewhere," Dad requested in a firm, tired voice.

"Where should I take him?" Tab answered trying not to giggle.

"Anywhere, just not here," Uncle Dave yelled in frustration.

Todd started down the stairs with poor Lightning following behind him. He decided not to tell his uncle that Lightening had drunk from the toilet not his water dish. Tab locked the pup in the ski rental room as his Uncle Dave walked to the bathroom mumbling, "Why me? Why me? Why do these dogs always come to me?"

Buddy, Todd, and Toni crawled deeper into their sleeping bags so Buddy's dad would not hear them as they giggled more while he kept mumbling "Why me?" Little Bear snuggled as close to Buddy as possible. The pup did not want to spend the rest of the night in the ski rental room with Lightning. Buddy and his three cousins drifted off to sleep with big smiles on their faces and Little Bear pushed in as closely as possible to Buddy.

Morning arrived quickly. It was hard to believe the visit had passed so quickly. It was time to go back home. Dad wanted to get an early start so he could beat the traffic on the interstate highway.

"I hope it's not two years before we see each other again," Buddy's mom said as she hugged Mary.

"Yeah, it's your turn to come visit us," Buddy's dad told Aunt Mary as he gave her a good-bye hug.

"I just can't seem to drag Rob away from the mountain."

"Well maybe you and the kids need to tie him up while he is sleeping, load him into your minivan, and bring him down to see us," Buddy's dad said, winking at Mary and the kids.

"We might just do that!"

The kids laughed, as each one pictured their dad tied up in the back of the van behind the bench seat as they headed down the highway to visit Buddy and his parents.

That scenario would have trouble matching this real story, however. Several years ago Uncle Rob, Aunt Mary and the kids were coming home from visiting Uncle Rob's parents in central Pennsylvania. It was about nine o'clock when Uncle Rob stopped for gas and went into the mini market. The kids joined him in the mini market while Aunt Mary was sleeping on the back seat of the van.

Little did they know that Aunt Mary went to the restroom while Uncle Rob was paying for the gas and the kids were picking out some snacks? When they returned from the market they buckled their seatbelts and continued driving home. This was before everyone had cell phones. No one missed Aunt Mary until they were home and began unpacking the luggage. When they finally realized what happened they had to travel over 75 miles back to the gas station to pick her up.

Uncle Rob and Jerry were already heading off in the old pickup truck to do some chores as Buddy's dad tooted good-bye on their van horn. On their way out of the lodge parking lot, Buddy could see the cloud of oily smoke coming from Old Smelly Belly's exhaust pipe (that is the nickname that the kids gave to the old truck) as it disappeared over the hill toward the top of the ski trail.

"Well, I wonder how long it will be before we see them again," Mom remarked as they pulled onto Route 22, heading for Interstate 84.

"It's a good thing we didn't feed Little Bear this morning," Mom said cautiously. "We sure don't want him to get carsick on the way home, do we, Dave?" Dad just shook his head frowned and didn't answer.

Buddy kept his fingers crossed during the entire trip. There were no incidents in the van this time, even though Buddy occasionally reached over, petted Little Bear, and secretly slipped him a doggie biscuit.

CHAPTER TWELVE

CHRISTMAS MISCHIEF

It was a great summer, but it passed too quickly. Buddy was back in school before he knew it. How is it that the summer vacations fly by so fast while school days and weeks seem to drag on and on? Buddy's new homeroom teacher and science teacher was Mr. Hoenscheid, a brand-new teacher. Mr. "H," as the kids quickly dubbed him, had attended Washington Middle School as a child, and has now returned as a teacher. Buddy's dad had been one of Mr. H's teachers back when Mr. H. was an eighth grader. Mr. H has adopted many of Buddy's dad's teaching methods and policies, including no tests on Mondays, which has made him very popular with the students.

Fall passed by as rapidly as the summer had, and now it was mid-December. Little Bear had grown at a fast pace. His ears were beginning to stand up straight like a German shepherd's ears. His fur color had changed from dark brown to red and medium brown. His tail was long like that of a red fox, but it lacked the white tip common to the red fox. He looked rather majestic, sporting a mane of fur around his neck like a male lion.

Little Bear was almost ten months old. According to the scale at the vet's office, he weighed sixty-five pounds--a far cry from the four pounds he had weighed when Buddy found him. He had quickly outgrown his first kennel. Buddy was excited because Dad and Little Bear were finally beginning to bond. In fact, Dad often played with the pup when he came home from school. Mom took a photo of Dad and the pup sitting on the kitchen floor; both decked out in sunglasses, and added it to her photo album.

It was hard to believe that Little Bear was the same pup Buddy had found on that cold February afternoon. It was still a mystery how Little Bear had ended up in the weed field in the middle of a cold winter afternoon, and as yet, no one had been able to identify his breed or combination of breeds.

Mom finished the Christmas shopping two weeks before the big day. All the unwrapped packages sat out in the open on the cedar chest at the foot of the bed in Mom and Dad's bedroom. In previous years, Mom had hidden the gifts in the spare bedroom closet, but she no longer needs to hide them from Buddy. She knows he will not snoop to see what is in the packages because of what had happened last year. The incident had ruined the excitement of Christmas Day for Buddy.

Several days before Christmas, Buddy's friend Rory Bradley had called to tell Buddy that he had found all his Christmas gifts hidden in the family's guest bedroom closet and no one was home. Rory had invited Buddy to come over and visit to play with the Christmas toys.

The two boys had had a great time. The gifts included a large remote-control bulldozer, several video games, and other items from Rory's Christmas wish list. There were also boxes containing new underwear, socks, and pajamas in a boy's size, but for some strange reason, the boys left those boxes untouched.

They had taken the toys downstairs and played with them in the living room. Rory had installed batteries so they could play with the bulldozer. Using the remote controls, they made the bulldozer push the bulldozer box around the living room. Rory went into the garage and brought in a bag of dry dog food and an old vinyl tablecloth.

They had poured a large pile of the dog food in the middle of the tablecloth and proceeded to take turns directing the bulldozer to scoop up the food and deposit it in a pan that Rory's mom used for baking brownies. Using another gift--a digital stopwatch--they had timed how long it took each one of them to place all the dog food in the pan.

Rory's dog, Hansy, hadn't understood that the dog food was not intended for him. Hansy, a buff colored cocker spaniel with long floppy ears, had tried to eat the food in the pan, so the boys used the bulldozer to chase him away. The game became even more fun as the boys teased Hansy with the bulldozer. In between the teasing, they continued to transfer the dog food from the tablecloth to the pan.

They had been having so much fun with the toys that they hadn't heard Rory's mother's car pull into the driveway, until she accidentally bumped the horn. Hansy began barking, as he always did when someone came into the driveway. Rory jumped up and looked out the window. His mom had already exited the car and was unloading packages from the back seat. Luckily, she had bought so many gifts that it would take awhile to unload them. She did not see Rory at the window.

"It's my mom! Quick, help me put everything back in the boxes," Rory had shouted. Buddy had just finished using the bulldozer to place the last pieces of dog food into the brownie pan. The two boys grabbed the bulldozer, the watch, and the other toys, as well as the boxes, lids, and tissue paper.

Somehow, neither boy had noticed that the directions sheet for the toy bulldozer was lying on the floor between the sofa and the coffee table. Leaping two steps at a time, they flew upstairs to the guest room. Rory had repacked the boxes while Buddy placed the lids on the top of each package. They stacked the boxes in the closet. Then the boys ran to Rory's bedroom, pretending that they had been there all the time.

"I hope my mom doesn't notice that the boxes aren't in the same positions as when she put them in the closet."

"Do you really think she would remember a little thing like that?"

"You don't know my mom as well as I do."

"Oh no," Rory had yelled! "We left the pan of dog food on the floor." Hansy was finishing the last morsel of food as Rory arrived in the living room. "I guess I won't have to feed you tonight," Rory told the pup as he put the brownie pan and the tablecloth in the garage and ran back to his bedroom. Hansy was at Rory's heels the whole way.

Buddy had scratched Hansy's ears as the boys and the pup lay on Rory's bed. "Boy, I hope I get a puppy for Christmas this year," Buddy commented as the doorbell rang.

Rory's mom had rung the doorbell, hoping someone was home that could help her. She hadn't wanted to put down the packages to unlock the door. Both boys ran down to meet her. Rory opened the door. Fortunately, the stack of boxes she was holding blocked her view of the bulldozer directions lying on the floor. She came through the door and worked her way to the dining room table.

"Hi ... Mom, how... was your shopping ... trip?" Rory had asked, trying to catch his breath.

"Fine, but I hate all the traffic at the mall. Why are you out of breath?" she had asked, still holding the boxes. Just then, Buddy spotted the directions. He quickly backed over to the piece of paper and pushed it under the couch with the back of his foot. "Oh, Buddy and I were playing soccer with the sponge ball in my bedroom, then we ran down the steps to open the door for you," Rory had replied, finally able to talk again.

Buddy had seated himself on the couch, pretending to tie his sneaker lace, so that he could reach under the couch to retrieve the directions sheet. Mrs. Bradley still couldn't see him, due to the stack of packages in her arms.

"What did you buy today? Did you buy me anything?" Rory had said, trying to change the subject. Buddy moved back into the dining room. He passed the directions behind his back to Rory. Then Buddy stepped closer to Mrs. Bradley and offered to help her with the stack of packages. "Here, let me help you with the gifts," Buddy said. He stood on his toes and removed the top three boxes from the stack. Mrs. Bradley's eyes and round, rosy cheeks appeared above the remaining boxes.

"Oh, just some extra gifts for your sister and your dad. You're not getting anything this year," Rory's mom had answered with a smile. "By the way, where is Karen?" Buddy continued taking boxes from Mrs. Bradley and putting them on the dining room table.

"I guess she is still playing with Gwen and Louise at their house," Rory had answered.

Mrs. Bradley turned toward Buddy. "Thank you for helping me with my Christmas gifts, Buddy. You are a fine young man."

"Mom, I forgot something upstairs, I'll be right back," Rory had exclaimed suddenly. He took off up the stairs to stash the directions sheet back in the bulldozer box.

Meanwhile Buddy had kept Mrs. Bradley busy talking in the dining room. Buddy liked to talk with Rory's mom. She's an editor at a local publishing firm, and she always treats Rory's friends like young adults. She doesn't treat them like little kids. Buddy thinks she is very pretty. Her broad smile and rosy cheeks give the appearance that she is always in a good mood.

By the time Rory had bounced back down the stairs, the December sun was beginning to drop near the distant Blue Mountain. Buddy knew he had to get going in order to be home before dark. He said goodbye to Rory and Mrs. Bradley.

"You call me as soon as you get home so I know that you are okay. I hate when you young men are out at this time of the day!" Mrs. Bradley had said firmly as Buddy went out the front door.

"I will, I will," he had yelled as he grabbed his bike and headed home. "Wow, she called me a young man two times. Rory's mom is so nice," Buddy said to himself as he coasted down the driveway.

Buddy's mother had told him to be home before dark. The December wind's chill bit his face as he pedaled along the dirt road that wound through the tree farm. He and Rory used the old road as a shortcut when traveling back and forth between their houses. That way, they didn't have to ride along the shoulder of the busy state highway.

Buddy had stood up on his pedals as he zigzagged his way up the old lane. He saw the familiar V shape of a local flock of Canada geese silhouetted against the evening sky. The local goose population was rising. They were geese that did not migrate south in the winter. They remained in the local area feeding in harvested corn and soybean fields.

Buddy remembered Dad telling him about how people would take their children to ponds and streams to feed the geese during the summer. Dad said that this practice was not good for the geese, because the birds would learn to depend on the free handouts, and the younger geese would not learn how to find their own food. Also, it encouraged the geese to stay in the area rather than migrate and the bread was not a natural food source for geese.

When Buddy had traveled about halfway to the top of the hill, he could see the geese gliding into the unfrozen portions of Jake's farm pond. Legs forward and wings outspread; they seemed to be applying brakes as they landed on the water. Their honking sounded like a traffic jam on the four-lane highway near the mall. One goose misjudged the open area, landed on the ice and slid across the ice to the edge of the pond. The funny spectacle had produced a smile on Buddy's cold face.

Buddy had been glad to see his house as he wound through the paths in the backyard. He propped his bike against the wall of the garage and raced to the side door. Fumbling with his key in the cold mid-December afternoon air, he felt relieved when he finally entered the comforts of the warm kitchen. While rubbing his hands together to get the blood flowing, he had noticed a note from Mom on the kitchen table.

Buddy,

Dad and I are doing some extra Christmas shopping. Eat some cookies and have a cup of milk. I made a batch of Aunt Edna's date-and-nut cookies this morning. They are in Nana's antique cookie jar. Don't eat too many cookies and be careful not to drop the lid. We will be home about six o'clock.

Love, Mom

After Buddy had read the note he called Mrs. Bradley to assure her that he had arrived home safe and sound. Cookies filled the next part of his agenda. Milk and cookies made a great treat after the cold ride home. He warmed the milk in the microwave and stuffed the end of a soft, milk-soaked cookie in his mouth. Devouring the first cookie in several bites, he stuffed the whole second one in his mouth at one time.

After five cookies and another half cup of warm milk, flavored with Hershey's chocolate syrup, Buddy had headed up to his room. "Shou I or shoun't I?" he mumbled, with the fifth cookie stuffed in his mouth, knowing full well that it would be at least an hour until his parents would return from shopping.

Should he? Should he go search for his Christmas presents? He had never been tempted to look for his gifts before Christmas day before, but it had been *so* much fun playing with Rory's gifts. "Nah, he had thought. "The gifts won't be in an obvious place like the guest bedroom closet, like they were at Rory's house." But, when he opened the guest room closet, there they were: Hess Brothers' Department Store boxes filled with gifts lying there on the floor. Hess Brothers was the big department store in Allentown. The store was a favorite destination for the shoppers in the Lehigh Valley area.

The guest room in Buddy's house is where Nana and Pappy Sterner stay when they come to visit from Florida. Nana and Pappy were visiting for the holidays, but at that moment, they had been in town having dinner with old friends. No one had been at home except Buddy. The idea of snooping became more powerful. "Should I look in the boxes or not?" he had repeated to himself.

"I wonder if all parents hide Christmas gifts in the spare bedroom," Buddy had said to himself. "What if you don't have a spare room? Then where would gifts be hidden? If I have kids when I grow up and ever have to hide gifts, I will bury them in a treasure chest in the backyard. My kids will never find them there.

"First, I'll make a treasure map like the pirates do. Then I'll hide the map so no one can find it. Maybe I'll dig a hole and hide the map in a coffee can, and then I'll bury the can at the base of a tree. There's no way my kids will be able to find their gifts before I put them under the tree on Christmas Eve."

"Cuckoo!" The bird in the cuckoo clock had brought Buddy back from his pirate treasure adventure. It was five thirty. What should he do? The temptation had been too great, and Buddy snooped. He found in-line skates, a DVD player and several of his favorite movies, a bulldozer exactly like Rory's, as well as other gifts from his wish list. There were even several boxes of clothing.

He had imagined zooming down the driveway on the skates. In and out of the slalom gates, he gracefully carved his turns in the new Olympic sport. The crowd applauded his skills as he crossed the finish line well in front of his competitors.

CHAPTER THIRTEEN

A SAD CHRISTMAS

"Cuckoo, cuckoo, cuckoo, cuckoo, cuckoo, cuckoo!"

"Yikes, it's six o'clock already. How could the time have passed so fast?" Buddy had yelled out loud. Mom and Dad were due home any minute. Buddy managed to put all the gifts back the way he had found them.

The following two weeks had been terrible, even though no one suspected Buddy's snooping secret. It seemed to take forever for Christmas Day to arrive. He had wanted so badly to use the in-line skates, but he couldn't reveal the fact that he knew the contents of all the gifts in the closet. Plus, if he had used the skates anywhere except in the house, the wheels would become scuffed. He thought of using the DVD player too, but the player was sealed in bubble wrap packaging, and the disks were in cases covered with a thin transparent wrapper. The bulldozer was heavily packed in Styrofoam making it almost impossible to remove from the box.

When Christmas had finally arrived, Buddy knew exactly what each package contained by the shape of the box. He had to fake how surprised he was as he opened each gift. Later in the morning, when the gift opening was finished, he had felt so guilty that he had confessed to his parents and grandparents about peeking at his gifts. He told them that it had ruined his Christmas, and that is why Mom knows she will never need to hide Buddy's Christmas gifts again.

This year, Nana and Pappy Sterner arrived from Florida two days before Christmas. Buddy and Dad met them at the airport on Saturday. They had quite a few gifts in their carry-on bags and stored luggage.

Christmas Day was great. Buddy thought it was much better *not* knowing what was in the packages. With all the happy events, the day didn't seem like a Monday at all.

Buddy doesn't particularly like Mondays, because Monday usually means he has to go back to school. He especially hates Sunday nights. His stomach always bothers him on Sunday evenings.

Every time Buddy complains about Sunday nights and the thought of going to school the next day, Dad tells him that he has nothing to complain about. Dad would always add together the years he had spent in elementary school, high school, college, and graduate school, plus his years as a teacher, and tell Buddy how he should not complain. Buddy had only been in school for about six years, including his year of half-day kindergarten and this year's half-year of sixth grade that he had already completed.

"Don't complain until you've done the time!" Dad would say. "Think about Pop-Pop. He spent a total of fifty-two years in school."

But this particular Monday was different. There would be no school until a week from Wednesday. "Christmas vacations are great," Buddy thought. The turkey and stuffing baking in the oven were filling the house with wonderful aromas. His Christmas gifts were exactly what he had had on his wish list.

The family gift was a new computer with all the latest accessories. Dad and Pappy were in the room that Mom refers to as "Dad's Room," trying to download all the programs. Mom's brother Bob would be arriving early to help set everything into motion on the computer. Mom and Nana were busy working in the kitchen. Nana's famous potato-bread stuffing and the smells of the turkey baking were making Buddy's mouth water. He was helping by washing and cutting vegetables for the relish tray when he decided he would rather go hiking with Little Bear. He washed his hands while Mom continued feeding cabbage into the food processor to make homemade coleslaw.

"Is it okay if I take Little Bear for a walk? We will be back before it's time to eat," Buddy yelled in the direction of his mom. He didn't wait for an answer. He grabbed his ski coat and hat from the laundry room closet and headed to the side door. Little Bear had been developing a vocabulary of words he recognized, especially the words "go" and "walk." He knew they meant he was going to go outside. The pup was running behind Buddy on the way to the side door. Securing the purple leash to Little Bear's choke chain, Buddy opened the door leading to the yard.

Mom was busy making her homemade coleslaw, but like most mothers, she was never so busy that she did not hear what her son said. "Don't be late; we will be eating in about two hours. Be careful!" She shouted over the whirling sound of the food processor.

"I'll be home in time," he yelled back, as Little Bear practically pulled him through the doorway. The pup was getting so strong that Buddy often had a hard time holding onto the leash when they went for a walk.

Hiking down through the Christmas tree farm, toward the same spot where Buddy first found Little Bear back in February, he noticed that the sky was becoming streaked with high cirrus clouds. He knew the high, featherlike cirrus clouds were an indication that bad weather would soon follow. "I hope the clouds don't turn into nimbus clouds. Then there might be rain or snow. Hey, I actually remember something from the weather unit lessons," he said, with a big smile on his face. The pup was wagging his tail and looking up at Buddy, as if wondering what he was talking about.

Little Bear began to tug on the leash. He must have smelled something and wanted to investigate. Buddy had to muster all his power to restrain the pup as they walked over the wet ground. If a rabbit or something else attracted the pup's attention, he would pull even harder.

Suddenly, Buddy caught a glimpse of a form about the size and color of a red fox running into the thick brush to his left. It was about thirty yards away. He only saw it for a second, but Little Bear was already pulling in that direction.

Trying to hold on, Buddy slipped on a patch of hard snow. He looked like a beginning water-skier trying to stay balanced on the water. Buddy's feet flew out from under him. As he fell with a thud, the loop of the leash pulled loose from his fingers. Little Bear charged off, the purple leash dragging behind him, in the direction where the foxlike creature had disappeared. Before Buddy could scramble to his feet, the pup was out of sight.

Buddy quickly followed, tracking the prints in the snow and mud. It was not a white Christmas, but a few areas of snow still remained in shaded areas from a light snow that had fallen the previous week. Buddy yelled and whistled, but Little Bear did not return. Many types of tracks intersected in the patches of snow and in the mud near the stream. Buddy followed each set of tracks, but all were dead-ends. None led to the missing pup.

Buddy searched for about an hour before running home. It was almost time for the big Christmas feast. Other family members would be arriving soon. Buddy was crying and shivering as he burst through the side door.

"Little … Bear… ran away," Buddy cried out, trying to regain his breath. He was hyperventilating from running. Plus, he was so upset about Little Bear running away that he could barely speak He sank to his knees on the dining room floor. Struggling to be understood, he managed to blurt out, "Little Bear ran after what I think was a red fox. I couldn't find him anywhere! I looked for about an…"

Dad interrupted, "We'd better go look for him right away. Maybe we can find him if we leave right now." Dad grabbed the van keys and his ski jacket. Pappy and Nana grabbed their coats and followed Dad to the garage. Mom turned down the settings on the stove and oven to low before grabbing her coat and scarf.

They drove along the country roads that surrounded the tree farm and old weed fields. The inside of the van windows were covered with moisture from their body heat and breath. They rubbed off the moisture as they tried to peer out the windows. About a half hour passed when Mom realized that it was getting late.

"I have to get back and finish dinner before the turkey and the rest of our food are ruined," Mom explained. "Uncle Queeny and Aunt Dorothy always come early, and Uncle Bob is coming to work on the computer. Someone needs to be there when they arrive," she continued.

"Take me home. The rest of you can keep searching," Nana interrupted as she wiped condensation from the window with her embroidered handkerchief. "You continue searching and I'll take care of dinner and welcome the guests."

"Thanks, but I want to be there," Mom answered firmly.

"I'll take you both home. We really don't need five people in the van. As long as we can watch both sides of the road, we should be okay. We'll be home in time for dinner and we will bring Little Bear with us," Dad said in a positive tone. Buddy forced a smile, trying not to start crying again.

Dad drove Mom and Nana home. Buddy, Dad, and Pappy continued searching through the neighborhood in the van. They stopped and asked neighbors if they had seen Little Bear. First, they asked a small neighbor boy who was running around in his front yard tossing a football in the air.

It was Little Billy. Buddy knew him because he rides to school on Buddy's bus. His father's name is Billy, so they call him Little Billy.

"Did you see my puppy anywhere?" Buddy yelled through the van window.

"Nope!" Little Billy yelled back as the football slipped through his hands. "I wasn't looking for no pup. Can't you see I've been busy scoring touchdowns all morning?"

"Well, please keep an eye open for him!"

"I will! I'll keep both eyes open."

Dad drove on down Friars View Drive. Even with the heartache of losing Little Bear, Buddy's thoughts began to wander. "Why do dads like to name their kids the same name? Then they call them Little Billy or Little Joe. It's not a good idea, because the 'little' part never goes away."

"Everyone still calls Dad's friend's son 'Little Gene,' and he is all grown-up and pretty old. He must be twenty-five and seven feet tall by now. What if Dad's name was Buddy, and they called me Little Buddy? When I'm real, real old--like maybe thirty-five--it would sound so dumb." He laughed to himself, thinking about the future. "And the winner of the Academy Award for best animal film goes to Little Buddy Sterner and his dog Little Bear," he imagined the announcer saying. "Calling me Little Buddy when I'm ancient, like in my thirties, sure would sound stupid." Buddy's daydreams helped him to forget his troubles for a little while.

Suddenly, the van came to a stop. Buddy snapped out of his daydream, hoping that Dad had stopped because he had spotted Little Bear.

Unfortunately, Dad had stopped the van only in order to pull into Mr. William's driveway. The neighbor was tinkering with a large gray snow blower near the entrance to his garage.

"Our dog is missing. Did you see him anywhere this morning?" Dad yelled through the open van window.

"What's that?" Mr. Williams yelled back over the idling engine of the snow blower.

Dad yelled again. "Did you happen to see our dog?"

Mr. Williams turned off the snow blower, and Dad asked for the third time. "Have you seen Little Bear? He is missing. Buddy was hiking in the tree farm earlier today. The pup pulled loose and ran off."

"Can't say I have, of course I wasn't paying any attention. I've been getting this new snow blower ready. I heard the Weather Channel was predicting a big storm later today. Isn't this machine a beauty?"

"Well, it's definitely a big one! If you see the pup, please give us a call." Dad wrote their phone number on a gasoline receipt he found on the floor of the van. He thanked Mr. Williams and carefully backed out of the driveway. "I'll be sure to keep an eye out for him," Mr. Williams shouted as he pushed the starter button on the snow blower.

Buddy shouted Little Billy's idea to Mr. Williams. "Please use both eyes!"

The search continued. Driving throughout the area, the search crew questioned everyone they saw out and about on the cloudy Christmas day. Unfortunately, no one had seen the pup. Most of the neighbors know the Sterners and Little Bear, so the searchers felt fairly certain that the pup was not in the immediate area. Someone would have seen him. A half-hour later, the search van returned to the Sterner's driveway. Dad pressed the remote for the garage door and carefully drove into the garage. Little Bear was still missing.

A few of Buddy's relatives had arrived for dinner. Buddy went from one to another, explaining how Little Bear had run away. It was evident to everyone that Little Bear was not there, because the pup would have barked his greeting as he drummed his long bushy tail against the washing machine and dryer each time the doorbell rang and someone approached the side laundry room door. As more relatives arrived, Buddy repeated his story. All the drivers agreed to join the search for the pup as soon as dinner was over.

It took about forty minutes for the nineteen-pound turkey to look as if a flock of buzzards had descended on it. The delicious golden brown Christmas turkey was reduced to bones and a few pieces of skin. There were still sweet potatoes and string beans, but all the other food was gone.

Buddy didn't have much of an appetite. It seemed like it took a hundred years until everyone finished with dessert and coffee. The usual chatting about what everyone had been doing over the past few months was about to begin when Buddy reminded the family about his urgent plea for everyone's help to search for Little Bear.

It was already three-thirty. There was less than an hour of daylight remaining. The drivers put on their coats and headed to their vehicles to begin the search. Little Bear had been missing since before noon. Mom, Nana, Mom-Mom, Pop-Pop, Aunt Helena and her friend Jim stayed behind to clear the table and take care of the dishes. Brad and baby Patrick took naps. Aunt Suzanne watched the other younger children as they played with their toys. Brad's older brothers, Jarod and Gary, went along with their dad, Uncle Don, to search for Little Bear.

The vehicles searched the back roads, occasionally passing each other, but no one had any good news. Dark clouds covered the late afternoon sky, and the searchers were rapidly running out of daylight. Uncle Queeny pulled up next to Uncle Bob's car in his big new Cadillac.

Buddy was riding with Uncle Bob, but no one was riding with Uncle Queeny because of his fat cigars. A big, stinky cigar dangled from Uncle Queeny's mouth as he described what he had seen. As usual, it was difficult to understand him with the cigar dancing between his teeth and the smoke circling his head, but it sounded like, "I saw some deer, but no dog."

Buddy chose to ride with Uncle Bob because he likes the gizmos that Uncle Bob buys. Uncle Bob is a bachelor and recently bought a new hybrid car. It gets 80 miles to the gallon, and it looks like a silver space mobile from a cartoon show like the Jetsons. It automatically turns off when you come to a stop sign or traffic light. This helps save gas while you are sitting in traffic and not moving. It also causes less air pollution. Buddy's family is very concerned about pollution and the environment.

As the early cirrus clouds had foretold, the weather was turning harsher. Just before dark it started to sleet. Uncle Bob and Buddy headed back to Buddy's house before his dad and Pappy returned. Bob pulled into the garage to wipe off his new car. The roads were getting slick, and the visiting relatives needed to head for their own homes before the roads became worse. One by one they came back to the house, gathered their belongings and departed for home.

CHAPTER FOUTEEN

THE SEARCH CONTINUES

"If we don't find your pup tonight, I'll stay overnight so we can look for him again first thing tomorrow morning. That way my new car will stay clean, too," Uncle Bob said as he wiped the final drops of moisture from the hood and roof. Uncle Bob carefully backed out of the garage as Dad pulled into the driveway. Buddy quickly helped Uncle Bob cover the car with a vinyl tarp.

Uncle Bob's decision to stay and help made Buddy feel a little better. Mom, Dad, Uncle Bob, and Buddy searched with flashlights for about an hour after everyone else had gone home. The weather became much worse. The valley where Little Bear had disappeared filled with a thick layer of fog. It was hard for the searchers to see each other as they walked back to the house.

That night Buddy had no desire to use the new computer or to play with his Christmas gifts. Dad tried to take Buddy's mind away from Little Bear by suggesting that they play Monopoly, Buddy's favorite board game. Buddy, however, was not interested.

Sadly, he trudged up the eleven steps to his bedroom. The realities of the day's events were catching up with Buddy. The steps seemed more like a mountain than a stairway. It was the worse Christmas ever. He lay in bed staring at the glowing star stickers on the ceiling. He was awake for a long time—longer than he had been the night before, even though that had been Christmas Eve. (And every kid knows that it takes forever to fall asleep on the night before Christmas!)

When Buddy finally did fall asleep, he dreamed wonderful dreams about playing with Little Bear. They were playing soccer in the basement, and Little Bear was the goalie. The dog hardly ever allowed the ball to slip past and roll into the makeshift goal. In Buddy's dream, the pup was better than the goalie on the school soccer team.

All of a sudden, Buddy awoke and sat up in bed with a big smile on his face. His smile faded as he realized he had been dreaming and that Little Bear was still lost. "Why wasn't yesterday a dream?" Buddy said out loud as he pushed the blankets aside. Swinging his feet over the side of the bed, he continued thinking about his lost pup.

Buddy heard the bird in the dining room clock call five times to tell anyone who might be interested that it was five a.m. Everyone but Buddy was snuggled in their beds with visions of sugar plums dancing in their heads.

Buddy crept down the stairs to see if Uncle Bob was awake. "Fat chance," Buddy thought. He knew that Uncle Bob liked to stay in bed as long as possible. He even wears an eye mask without holes so that everything will remain totally dark no matter how late he sleeps.

Buddy sat quietly in the chair next to the daybed where his uncle lay snoring. Although he knew he should wait until Uncle Bob woke up on his own, Buddy could not resist poking his uncle gently in the ribs every few minutes, hoping he would stir from his deep hibernation. After each poke Uncle Bob rolled over, mumbled something indistinguishable, and then began snoring again.

Uncle Bob is definitely not a person who likes to get out of bed early. He takes after his older sister Elizabeth, Buddy's mom. She doesn't like to get up early either if she doesn't have to. Buddy poked Uncle Bob again. "Please wake up and help me start looking for Little Bear," Buddy said in a determined whisper. But it wasn't until the bird called once to indicate five-thirty that Uncle Bob finally responded to Buddy's requests.

"What time is it?" Uncle Bob asked, resting his head on one arm. Then he sat up, yawning and stretching his arms. He looked like a bandit in pajamas until he finally removed his eye mask and squinted at Buddy. "What time is it?" he asked again.

"Oh, somewhere around five-thirty."

"Five-thirty; are you crazy or something?" Uncle Bob blurted out.

"No, I'm not crazy. I couldn't sleep, so I came down to see if you will please help me look for Little Bear. Please, please, pretty please," Buddy begged.

"Well, okay. I'm awake now!" Uncle Bob said a bit disgustedly, as he stretched his long arms above his head. He shuffled his legs from under the covers and sat on the edge of the daybed.

"Time to search for Little Bear," Buddy said with a forced smile. "Get dressed and come upstairs. I'll make some coffee for you."

The sun was beginning to peek over the rolling hills to the southeast as Uncle Bob and Buddy started a new search. Fog continued to fill the valley. About an inch of sleet had fallen overnight, but the big storm that Mr. Williams had hoped for had not occurred. Small icicles had formed on the edges of roofs during the night. In spots where the sun pierced through the fog, the icicles took on the look of magical rainbow sticks aglow with light. It would have been a beautiful morning if only Little Bear had not run away.

The layers of sleet crunched under Buddy and Uncle Bob's feet. They walked together for about an hour, and then returned to the house. There were no signs of the pup.

Mom and Dad were sitting in the kitchen as Buddy and Uncle Bob entered from the side door. Mom felt helpless. She had to work a double shift at the hospital because she had not worked on Christmas Eve and Christmas Day. She would not be able to help look for Little Bear, and she had become very attached to the pup. After a quick breakfast, Mom left for work while Dad, Uncle Bob, and Buddy began driving around in the van looking for Little Bear.

The fog lifted as the sun began rising higher in the sky. The sleet covering the roads was melting from the warmth of the sun. Mist rose from the dark road surface in front of the van, making the road look like a giant hot frying pan beginning to cook.

First they drove north toward the mountain, and then they circled back on another road. They stopped to talk to everyone they saw, asking if anyone had seen a medium-size dog. Buddy was carrying a recent photo of Little Bear. There were a lot of visitors in the neighborhood for the holidays, so carrying the photo was a good idea, but no one had seen Little Bear.

They spotted Mr. Williams using his snow blower to remove the sleet that covered his driveway. Dad waved to him. "You didn't see Little Bear, did you?" Dad yelled through the open window of the van.

"What's that?" Mr. Williams yelled back as he cupped his left hand over his ear and turned the snow blower toward the van almost losing control. Wet sleet flew from the blower chute toward the van window. Dad quickly closed his window as Mr. Williams grabbed the snow blower firmly and struggled to redirect the chute.

"We're still searching for our missing pup. Have you seen him?" Dad yelled through a small opening in the window. Mr. Williams finally turned off the noisy snow blower. Dad felt it was safe to open his window and he repeated the question. "Have you seen Little Bear?"

"Nope, I'm sorry. I haven't seen him. Darn, I was hoping for a whopper of a storm so I could really dig this baby into the snowdrifts. Those doggoned weathermen. You just can't count on them to predict a good blizzard anymore."

Buddy's dad waved good-bye as they drove away from the driveway. Next, they parked the van and searched on foot. They walked through some small wooded areas and along the opposite sides of several tree lines. There were no signs of Little Bear. They searched back and forth through several harvested cornfields. Although a maze of deer tracks crisscrossed the fields, there were no tracks with claw marks at the front to indicate that a dog had been in the area.

Returning to the van, they continued their search along the country roads. As they rounded a bend near the old Kreidersville Covered Bridge, they saw two vehicles stopped in the road directly ahead of them. It looked like something was lying in the road in front of a pickup truck, which was facing in the same direction as Dad's van. A white minivan was facing them in the opposing traffic lane, just outside the entrance to the bridge next to the pickup truck. The hood of the truck was open and steam was rising into the cold morning air. The vehicles blocked the road, thus halting the searchers' progress. No one in the van said a word.

Dad shifted into reverse and looked over his shoulder for a safe place to park. Cautiously, he backed up until he found a clear area where the steep bank did not reach to the edge of the road. He carefully maneuvered the van and parked. They were about 150 yards away from the covered bridge. They could see two men standing in the road. The men were talking and gesturing, but it was difficult to see what was lying in the road beside them.

Dad, Uncle Bob, and Buddy walked slowly along the shoulder of the road in silence. When they were about fifty yards from the bridge, Buddy's heart almost stopped. There was a brown animal lying motionless on the road in front of the truck. Buddy's eyes filled with tears. He ran back to the van. Losing Little Bear would be more than he could stand. He blamed himself for not having a stronger grip on the leash.

As Dad and Uncle Bob approached the truck, they discovered that the brown shape lying on the road was a small deer. Apparently, it had traveled down the steep bank to the right of the road to get a drink from the stream. The deer had jumped out in front of the truck and was killed instantly when the truck hit it.

"All of a sudden, it was right in front of me! I couldn't stop." The driver of the pickup truck was very upset. "I didn't even have a chance to put on my brakes. It seemed to appear out of nowhere! I was hardly moving--I had already slowed down to enter the bridge." The man was so worked up that he seemed to be yelling instead of talking.

Uncle Bob sprinted back to the van. "Buddy, it's a young deer. It's not Little Bear!"

"Oh, thank you, thank you, thank you!" Buddy cried out. He was upset to hear that a young deer had been killed, but he was certainly relieved that it was not Little Bear lying motionless in the road. Buddy and Uncle Bob jogged down the road to join Dad by the bridge.

"There are entirely too many deer!" the driver said, looking in disbelief at the damage to the front of his vehicle. The collision with the deer had sprung the hood and punctured the radiator. Steam still filled the air above the truck engine and hot yellowish-green antifreeze dripped from a hole in the radiator.

"I know what you mean. My wife hit a deer with her car on MacArthur Road about two miles north of the mall last week. Thankfully she wasn't hurt," the minivan driver commented.

"Look at the damage to my truck. I bet my insurance is going to increase because of this!"

"Can we do anything to help?' Dad asked.

"No thanks. I called my wife. She's calling our insurance company, the local game commission officer, and Triple A.

"Good luck. I'm glad you're not hurt. By the way, you didn't see a small dog similar in color to this deer along any of the roads or in the fields? My son's pup ran away yesterday and we've been searching for him." Buddy quickly pulled the photograph from his pocket and showed it to the two men.

Both drivers answered no to the missing-pup question, but agreed to stay on the lookout for the pup.

The three searchers slowly walked back to the van. The white minivan driver tooted his horn as he cautiously drove by them. Dad slowly drove toward the bridge and carefully pulled around the pickup truck and the deer. As they headed into the dim light of the covered bridge, Buddy's thoughts drifted from his lost puppy to a school program last fall.

Officer Z had presented the assembly program. He told the teachers and students that over one hundred thousand deer had been killed on Pennsylvania highways during the year.

Officer Z had said that if there were no fall and early-winter hunting seasons to reduce the size of the deer herd in the state, then there would be many more vehicle-deer collisions each year. Many people do not understand that the deer hunting season is the best method for managing the large deer population. He also explained that when the deer population is too high, the young and weaker deer are not able to find enough food to survive through the winter, especially when there are periods of deep snow. The death of deer due to starvation becomes a terrible waste of a natural resource.

The van bounced along the back roads. "Do you know why the bridges are covered with a roof?" Dad asked Buddy and Uncle Bob. He hoped to take Buddy's mind off the missing pup, plus he never misses a possible teaching moment. Both Uncle Bob and Buddy said they thought it was to protect wagons and horseback riders from bad weather. "Well, if you happened to be near a bridge, the roof would help keep you dry, but actually, the bridges were built with roofs to protect the bridge itself from rain and snow. The wooden bridge surfaces lasted much longer when the bridges were covered. It was also dark enough for a young man to steal a kiss from his girlfriend as they passed through the bridge. Some people called the covered bridges kissing bridges."

The searchers continued to question everyone they encountered. They spotted deer in the fields and one along the edge of the road. Several times, what appeared to be Little Bear off in the distance proved to be just another deer. With a sigh, Dad said, "It's almost noon. Let's go home for lunch and plan our afternoon search."

"No, I don't want to go home. Let's keep searching. I'm not hungry anyway. Please, can't we just keep looking?" Buddy begged trying to convince Dad to keep going.

Dad was not deterred. "We need to eat something. Then we'll head right back out again and we'll find Little Bear. Why don't you make some lost puppy posters while I rustle something up for lunch? I promise you that we will go out again as soon as we eat."

Uncle Bob agreed. "Your dad's right. We need some food. I'm hungry and I know I'll be able to do a better job searching for Little Bear if I eat something. We'll all have more energy and we'll be more alert."

Buddy knew that Dad and Uncle Bob were right and that he had lost the battle to continue searching without a lunch break. "Okay, but no wasting time. We have to leave the house again by one o'clock," Buddy stressed.

CHAPTER FIFTEEN

HAPPY NEW YEAR

Buddy had no appetite, so while Dad and Uncle Bob ate lunch, he began making posters to place at local businesses. He used a black marker to write LOST DOG in big letters on pieces of poster board. He made extra copies of a photo of Little Bear on the computer printer and glued one onto each poster and printed his address and phone number under each Little Bear photo.

"Buddy, get in here and eat something. You can't go searching the rest of the afternoon on an empty stomach," Dad insisted.

Buddy rinsed down one half of a grilled cheese sandwich with a glass of milk and slurped a few spoonfuls of tomato soup. It was one o'clock. Dad backed the van out of the garage right on schedule. They stopped at several businesses to drop off Buddy's posters. The locations were the same businesses where Buddy and Dad had placed posters in February when Buddy found Little Bear. This time, though, Buddy had no plans to sneak back and remove the posters.

They put up five posters and questioned the business owners about Little Bear. On the way to Jake's farm to drop off the last poster, Dad explained how he planned to use a search-and-rescue technique that he had learned when he was a member of the National Ski Patrol. He described how the search members spread out in a straight line across the area to be searched. Each searcher must keep the person on the left and right in sight as the team moves ahead, so no areas are missed during the search. The group proceeds forward slowly, looking side-to-side and ahead while trying to walk in a straight line.

Dad had called their neighbor, Mr. Ronchar, from home to see if he was available to join in the search. Luckily he was available and agreed to meet them at the tree-farm parking lot. He brought his two yellow Labs, Barney and Gradey. Dad figured that the hunting dogs might be able to track Little Bear's scent using Buddy's baby blanket. Little Bear still slept on the blanket every night.

Jake had promised to keep his eyes open for Little Bear while he did his farm chores. Now that Christmas was over, he was cleaning up from the hectic weeks of Christmas tree sales.

As the members of the search crew met in his parking lot, Jake decided to forget his farm chores for a bit and join in the search, too. Jake had grown quite fond of Little Bear. Buddy and his pup stopped by the farm quite often to visit Jake and help him with his chores. Little Bear was always very well behaved around Jake's farm animals.

Mr. Ronchar held Buddy's baby blanket in front of his dogs. It was clear that the scent was familiar to them. They made excited yipping sounds and madly wagged their tails. The two dogs strained against their leashes pulling in the direction toward the area where Little Bear had disappeared. Dad quickly explained the search-and-rescue method to Jake and Mr. Ronchar. The group spread out in a line, with Mr. Ronchar and the dogs in the middle. The dogs led the search team off toward the stream.

They found Little Bear's purple collar and leash on the other side of the stream near the top of the hill, next to an old stone row, where farmers had once piled stones unearthed by their plows. The rabies tag and the identification tag with Little Bear's name and the Sterner's phone number were still attached to the collar. The loop of the leash was caught on an old rotting stump root. It appeared as though Little Bear had struggled to free himself until the collar's buckle finally had broken open.

Buddy's spirits sagged as he examined the torn collar and leash. Without the identification tag, no one would know how to return the pup. Quietly, except for the panting and occasional yipping from Barney and Gradey, the search party continued their quest. After about two hours of searching the tree farm and two neighboring farms, the searchers circled back to Jake's parking lot. Jake needed to get back to his post-holiday cleanup chores.

The familiar figure in the red coat and hat disappeared behind the warehouse. Mr. Ronchar loaded his dogs into his sport-utility vehicle and said good-bye. Dad and his two passengers followed Mr. Ronchar out of Jake's parking lot and headed home. The state highway was busy with rush-hour traffic.

When they got home, Buddy sat in the living room staring out the window. He pictured in his mind how Little Bear and Gradey often played together. Gradey was older and more aggressive. He would grab Little Bear's leash and drag the pup around the yard growling and yipping, hoping that the younger pup would chase him in return. Finally, Little Bear would begin participating in the game. Round and round the yard they would dart, first Little Bear chasing Gradey, then Gradey turning around to chase Little Bear.

Mr. Ronchar has a small orchard at the back of his yard on the other side of the tree farm. Buddy had often hiked down to Mr. Ronchar's so the pups could play. What fun the pups had chasing, rolling, and growling through the orchard. Barney was older and did not enjoy the rough play. He usually gave a short growl to let Gradey and Little Bear know he would rather sit under one of the orchard trees and rest in the shade.

The visions of Little Bear and Gradey romping together brought tears to Buddy's eyes. How could they have failed to find the lost pup, even with Dad's special search-and-rescue technique and the help of the keen noses of Mr. Ronchar's dogs? Little Bear was still missing!

Dad, Uncle Bob, and Buddy searched on foot until it was too dark to see. Uncle Bob decided to stay overnight again.

Wednesday morning arrived quickly. Buddy was so tired from the previous day's search that he slept very soundly. In fact, Uncle Bob had to poke Buddy in the ribs to wake him. Uncle Bob had to go to work. Mom had a day off after her double work shift, so she took Uncle Bob's place on the search team. As Uncle Bob headed down the hill in his space-mobile car, the new search team organized.

Buddy explained to Mom, "I guess if Little Bear had to get lost, it's a good thing it happened during the holidays and not during a regular school week. This way we have the time to search for him." It was odd logic, but it made Buddy feel a little better.

School was closed until the following Tuesday, and more people volunteered to help search for Little Bear. Mr. Ronchar had the holiday week off from his job with the insurance company, so he brought his dogs to help again. Mr. Pete brought his dog, too. Buddy's friends Chris, Mike, and Gene also came to their friend's aid. Part of the four Musketeers' code was to always help a Musketeer in need.

Buddy hoped that such a large group would have better luck finding Little Bear. They continued to use Dad's search-and-rescue method. There were many open fields and wood lots to search between the place where Little Bear had disappeared and the Blue Mountain. It was too large an area to search properly, but the group intended to do their best to cover as much territory as possible.

"He probably wandered north toward the mountain," Mr. Ronchar commented as he opened the back of his vehicle. Barney and Gradey jumped down. They were ready to get back to work.

"Thanks for helping," Buddy told Mr. Ronchar, bending down to let the dogs lick his face.

"I'm happy to help. Besides, I don't get much chance to work the dogs during the cold winter, so this is good exercise for the dogs and me."

Dad interrupted. "There are fewer people between here and the mountain, so I think we should begin searching in that direction." Mr. Ronchar and Mr. Pete agreed. They loaded their dogs into their vehicles and headed toward the Pennsylvania Game Commission's parking lot near Danielsville, where the Appalachian Trail crosses the road. The parking lot would be the starting point for the new search.

"I hope someone visiting here for Christmas didn't find Little Bear and take him home with them," Buddy said, his voice cracking as his eyes filled with tears. He feared that if the pup had wandered all the way to the Blue Mountain it would be practically impossible to find him.

Riding in the back of the van, Buddy started talking to himself. "What if someone from New York City found Little Bear? What if they took him to the city and they were TV-commercial producers and they made him a big TV star? He would become famous and have his own show. I wonder if he would want to come back with me if I went to New York to tell the new owners that he is my pup." All these crazy thoughts clogged his brain. Nearly three days had passed since Little Bear's disappearance.

"What are you mumbling about back there?" Mom inquired.

"Oh, nothing, I'm just talking to myself. Nothing important."

The search group did not find Little Bear on the mountain that day. The search continued for the rest of the week, with many volunteers joining the family to walk through fields and woods. It all seemed to be of no avail. Little Bear was nowhere to be found.

It was New Year's Eve: Six days had passed with no signs of Buddy's pup. Uncle Tom and Aunt Suzanne arrived with Buddy's cousins Jarod, Ryan, and Brad to celebrate New Year's Eve.

Although his older cousins were great fun, Buddy's four-year-old cousin Brad had become a royal pain in Buddy's neck. In fact, Buddy referred to him as "Brad the Brat."

Buddy was in no mood to celebrate the New Year. It had been a full week since Little Bear disappeared. Buddy continued to blame himself. "How can anyone be happy?" he thought. "A year that had been the best year of my whole life has turned into the worst year in the history of the world."

Uncle Tom and Aunt Suzanne were staying in the spare bedroom where Buddy had found his Christmas presents last year. Jarod and Gary were going to sleep in sleeping bags on the floor in Dad's office. When Mom informed Buddy that Brad was going to spend the night sleeping in Buddy's bed and that she wanted Buddy to sleep with his little cousin Buddy stomped off to the kitchen mumbling under his breath. "I can't believe Mom is doing this to me. The little brat plays with my toys without asking and does lots of other annoying things."

"Last year he broke my remote-control bulldozer on Christmas Day. I didn't even have a chance to play with it first. When he came to visit on Easter Sunday, he covered Little Bear with Mom's shampoo. On the Fourth of July he threw my baseball cap in the toilet and flushed it. Then on Thanksgiving he pulled on the end of tablecloth at the kids' table and all the food landed on my lap. Man, I could go on and on." Buddy liked to play with Jarod and Gary, but having the Brat around was sure to make a bad time even worse. "I think I'll grab some cookies, disappear to my bedroom, and lock the door so the Brat can't get in."

"Where are you going?" Dad asked when he found Buddy sneaking out of the kitchen with a plate of Christmas cookies and a glass of milk.

"I'm going to bed. I don't feel like celebrating. I have a bellyache."

"If you have a bellyache, why do you have a plate full of Aunt Edna's cookies?"

Buddy couldn't think of a good answer to the question, so he didn't answer.

"I know you are very upset about Little Bear. We all feel badly and miss him, but you are going to act like a grown-up and spend the evening with the family. You are not going to your room! Do you understand me?" Dad said firmly. "It's only eight o'clock. Go offer your cousins some cookies and milk." Dad went back into the living room.

"Oh great," Buddy said under his breath. "Ten more seconds and I would have escaped to my room. Now I guess I'm supposed to serve the little monster and everyone else some cookies with a pretend smile on my face like I'm having fun or something."

Just then Brad popped into the kitchen singing, "Buddy is a big fat dope. Buddy is a big fat dope." Brad sang loudly as he marched around the kitchen table with a noisemaker in his right hand and a pointed silver hat on his head. He marched by Buddy and grabbed two cookies from the plate with his left hand.

Aunt Suzanne entered the kitchen. "Are you boys having fun?" she asked. Buddy just stood there and rolled his eyes. Brad continued marching around the kitchen table. Finally he went out through the kitchen door into the dining room. Aunt Suzanne smiled, thanked Buddy, took the plate of cookies from his hand, and followed Brad into the dining room.

Buddy was so angry that he didn't even want to play with Jarod and Gary. "Why did they have to come to visit tonight? Don't they know what happened this week?" Buddy began thinking of clever ways to keep Brad quiet in case he did encounter him again.

"Maybe I could give him several real marshmallows, and then convince him that my white pillow is a giant marshmallow. If I can get Brad to eat the pillow it will keep him from talking or singing the rest of the night."

Buddy ran to his bedroom and grabbed his pillow, then headed to the living room to join the family. Thankfully, Buddy didn't have to try his plan, because Brad the Brat fell asleep before nine o'clock.

Buddy felt that this was the longest night of his life. Finally, midnight approached. Everyone was sitting in the living room in front of the TV, wearing stupid pointed hats, waiting for the big light-bulb–covered ball in Times Square in New York City to drop marking the end of the old year and the beginning of the new one.

"Sixty, fifty-nine, fifty-eight, fifty-seven, fifty-six. Come on everyone, help me count!" Dad yelled out. It was Dad's idea to count down the last minute of the year on New Year's Eve. Would it also be the longest minute of Buddy's life?

"Thirty-seven, thirty-six, thirty-five," everyone was singing out the seconds.

Buddy was sitting on the edge of the living room recliner near the hallway with his arms folded, refusing to count. He was about to put the pillow he had intended for Brad over his own head to cover his ears. He needed to block out these sounds of family merriment at the end of the worst year in the history of the world. But as he lifted the pillow, he thought he heard faint scratching sounds at the front door.

Buddy strained his ears, hoping to hear the sound again. Yes, it definitely sounded like something scratching the door. No one else heard, because they had their eyes and ears glued to the TV and were intently counting down the seconds.

Much like Santa in the "Night Before Christmas," Buddy sprang from his chair to see what was the matter. And there at the front door, on the new fallen sleet, was the very best little New Year's treat.

Yes, standing on the porch, covered with burrs and soaked to the skin, looking more like a drowned rat than Buddy's pretty pup was none other than Little Bear. It was the best sight Buddy had ever seen. His fabulous Christmas gifts couldn't compare to the one that had just arrived at the door.

The ball had landed, and everyone was hugging and kissing each other in the living room as part of the New Year's celebration. The rest of the family did not realize there was another special celebration going on in the hallway at the front door. Buddy sat on the floor and started hugging the wet, burr-covered pup. He was giving him the biggest hugs and kisses he had ever given to anything or anyone in his life.

"Where have you been all week? You had me so worried. I was afraid I would never see you again. I'm so glad that you're back." Tears filled Buddy's eyes. He was so happy.

Usually when Buddy tried to give Little Bear a hug, the pup struggled to pull away. Not this time! Little Bear had jumped right into Buddy's lap. The pup could not get close enough. His tail was wagging faster than Barbara Corbo's tongue flapped when spreading some good gossip. Buddy got on his knees and took hold of the pup's front legs. They swayed back and forth performing a homecoming celebration dance.

Little Bear wagged his tail and did a little puppy dance all by himself on his back legs. The hugging and dancing in the hall continued until well after the celebration in the living room had settled down. Buddy was almost as wet as the pup. Sticky burrs were hanging from his new sweater.

Buddy finally picked up the wet pup and ran into the living room, shouting as loud as he could. "HAPPY NEW YEAR! HAPPY NEW YEAR, EVERYONE! Look who was at the door?" Everyone yelled Little Bear so loudly that Brad sat up and began crying. Buddy was so happy that he even gave Brad a big hug and a kiss on the top of his head while wishing him a Happy New Year.

"Hey, you're wet and your dog stinks!" Brad cried out.

"Happy New Year, everyone," Buddy repeated giving Little Bear another big hug. Everyone agreed it was a wonderful New Year's Eve.

But where was Little Bear? It looks like the mystery of Little Bear will continue!

Not quite the end!